Angelica

Angelica

A SENSUAL ROMANCE

Leo Birch

Full Court Press
Englewood Cliffs, New Jersey

First Edition

Copyright © 2024 by Leo Birch

Published in the United States of America by Full Court Press, 601 Palisade Avenue, Englewood Cliffs, NJ 07632
fullcourtpress.com

PRINT ISBN 978-1-953728-30-2
EBOOK ISBN 978-1-953728-34-0
Library of Congress Control No. 2024906702

Editing and book design by Barry Sheinkopf

TO LOLA

PREFACE: ANDES TREES

T HERE IS COMFORT IN A LIFE ALREADY LIVED. Having read the books, having felt the skin of joy and the despair of loss. All the mistakes that were made are done and cannot be retrieved.

In the garden of the house upstate, amidst the Catskill Mountains, there are but only a few trees. A few are tall and large, thick trunks with bark that cracks. Refuge for birds that seek a station in their short existence. Good trees, with room for nests, and insects that crawl upon them. Big trees that witness floods, and snow storms and kids that grow up as they run around them, or even swing on their limbs on homemade wooden planks tied to the branch with that special knot that lets it all happen smoothly. And then there are the smaller trees that were planted back in the yesteryears. . . .

He takes a step back, and then a few more. So easy to get lost within the tangle of branches when he prunes the limbs from within the aura of the crab apple trees. They were planted for his sons several seasons ago. The older Indian gardener takes care of them throughout the year and they have thrived through the treacherous cold that can make wood snap, and the wind that can take trees down like a piece of paper in the hand of fate. But he himself never actually spent much time on them. He never stayed at the house long enough to do so.

He had to first see them. Not just as the space occupying objects that divide the property between their house and the neighbors, but intrinsically as objects in space, standing by themselves, spanning the full circumference of their stand. Limbs shooting all around to create a vast ball of branches rich with life.

He first bought the long red clippers. It has handles that tel-escope out and allow him to reach the taller branches and, by strength of the lever action, the thicker ones as well. It is a great tool, well-designed and sharp, but there are just so many different branches even in the small trees. So he bought a smaller hand-held clipper that allowed him to get in closer con-tact with each branch and find their inner rhythm of growth. How the under-branches were growing away from the celebra-tion of leaves and light. And how the inner leaders were grow-ing straight up, mimicking the mother trunk but with none of its glory; just taking a shortcut to the top and hence crossing other branches and messing up their original path. And in that atmosphere of living force, of buds about to explode in white flowers, he let himself be the judge of which branch would stay and which would go. Like a Kol Nidre of sorts. It was all new to him. But soon enough it became obvious that even if mistakes were made, new seasons would bring new life, and the overall shape of the tree would not be affected by a few cuts too many.

He stepped out and looked from afar and saw a pattern within the crossing of the twigs and branches. In that maze he found windows of light, and snapping away he let the trees breathe from within and all around. A sphere of orchestrated beauty. He took a few steps back and, with his hands, raised from afar, he followed the edge of the trunk and the thicker lower branches. *Comme un chef d'orchestre.* The whole tree becoming a musical composition, with areas of dense energy and then quiet harmony. He left some twisted branches down low to remind him of humble beginnings and allowed windows of light to appear at eye level, leaving the top crown blossom out of reach of even his longest clippers. Ha! If life could be so simple, and to be able to cut away into its fabric and shape its future. The allegory of the son's trees and their life an indeniably sweet and sugary one to do. But our life is not like trees, or at least not exactly. Yet from the tree we can take the sap. That fantastic inner source of energy that re-mains dormant during winter and flows upward, like rain from within, at spring time. May that sap be in us. And let it allow us to grow all around; not just ahead of our eyes, but circumferentially, with branches sprouting from our back and shoulders like wings. Our minds expanding in a sphere with the radiance of everything surrounding us, hovering around us, in unison.

Some branches need to be stopped. They lead us to places we do not need to be. They suck the vital energy, and on these apple trees he cut them off, letting the sap feed exclusively the tip of the remaining extended branches. He also took down most of the deadwood, there seemed no need to carry that weight.

Sometimes a smaller branch would bounce up higher when the dark and dead limbs were removed. It became easier to recognize which branches were dead or not as the early buds started to grow and life revealed itself again.

He looked at the trees in the early hours of the day, and when the sun set along them. And by chance, when days were about to get warmer, he once saw the fullness of the trees in a freak squall of snow. A perfect moment when the tree became white with light at its core and the yet unfolded green leaves were just about to curl out. Pristine harmony of a living perfection. The bliss of life that summons from all over to persist, and endure, and give back.

ONE

ANGELICA STEPPED INTO THE SHOWER, closed the glass door behind her, and walked into the already-running water. It was set just right, and it flowed deliciously over her nakedness, away from all eyes. All she wanted to do was to rinse off the residue from the bath, the soapiness that clung to her, the foam bubbles that lingered like lace along her slender waist, and the remains of his sperm still spread upon her face and neck. Her lips were sealed even as the water streamed down her raised face. It was smooth and soft and warm. She kept her arms outstretched in front of her, against the hotel's black marble shower wall, allowing the water to bounce off her neck and her full breasts in a myriad of beads that captured the light. And then, giving up, she bowed her head and let the stream penetrate her hair as well. All noise disappeared. All feelings gone, too. Gone was the taste of Jim as the water made its way through her lips and into her mouth, and with it, gone as well the memory of most of it. She was okay with that. She did not need to remember every detail of their last few moments together.

Actually, she quite enjoys forgetting. It gives her pleasure, as if it leaves more room for other memories to appear, to happen. Like emptying a cup and waiting for it to be filled up again. She brought her head up and the water bounced into the back of her mouth. She was the one who had unfastened Jim's buttons and released him through the folds of his dark blue jeans. She had wanted to do it, ever since he brought her back to her suite after that crazy morning in Central Park.

She still could not believe what she had done just a few hours before. How could she let them handcuff her to the branch of the tree, almost naked, in the dark, cold morning air? The sunrise had finally brought redemption, for that was when the shot was taken. Strange that it's called a shot, she thought, as if it was coming from a gun. Yet instead of blood, it was a picture that blossomed in the light of dawn. In her mind, she re-created the image they had staged, and it was exactly what she had wanted. More than anything, she wanted to capture images of herself in a state of complete seduction regardless of what it took, regardless of whether she would be dominating or dominated, as long as it extended the essence that her soul demanded. And that soul was very demanding, for it trickled down through the ages to Aphrodite, one of the few original ones to populate the surface of Earth.

As for Jim, she had taken him in her mouth as a favor to him for having been so kind to her. For sheltering her, bringing her back all the way to her room, and running a hot bath for her. He had been surprisingly good. Solid, even. The way he understood her almost instinctively and cared for her, making sure she would not freeze out there in the cold, holding her tight in her sheared mink coat. She also loved that he unexpectedly took those last images of her, walking almost nude along Central Park, with her coat open just enough to reveal her translucent skin in the morning light.

Her strut had been somewhere between a walk of shame and the glorious apotheosis of a wild party. She had walked up tall, raised on her heels, a defiant smile on her face still pale in the cold, her lips crimson where she bit them. She knew what she was doing without having to think about it. It was predestined. Aphrodite, the goddess of seduction, was living in her, bringing up the clues and tricks and attitudes that made her whole. So, she had walked down the narrow Central Park alley towards his pointed camera, as if the world itself was her catwalk. She had walked as if she had always been meant to meet him on that path and, later, it did reveal itself on the final image. On it she projected allure and humility all at once. Her strength was evident in her ability to show her weakness. Like a Man Ray smile lost in the clouds, her red lips floated down the alley. She was not thinking of sex at that moment, just of floating. But if, right there in public, he had cupped her naked breasts with his large hands, she would have let him do it, and let him pinch her nipples tight in the cold as well.

Back in her suite, she had walked naked into the bathroom where he had been running her bath. He had tried to step out as she came in, but she held his hand and kept him close. He'd watched her step into the hot water, one foot at a time, her nakedness swallowed by the depth of the bubbles. Her face had relaxed as she let her head lean back against the heated porcelain tub. The back of her neck had matched the curve of the rim and her slender shoulders warmed under the envelope of hot water. She'd closed her eyes for an instant, enjoying every little pleasure her body offered her right at that moment. Only then had she realized that she was still holding onto his three middle fingers, like a toddler. With eyes still closed, she brought his thick fingers to her lips and inserted them into her mouth. She could taste him already. His scent. His vigor. And her desire.

She does these things easily.

Maybe because she forgets them easily.

THE NEXT MESSAGE CAME TO HER in the same light-blue box as the first one. This time it contained a vintage bracelet, flat and wide, made of thin gold links that molded themselves smoothly to her slender wrist. With it was a first-class plane ticket bearing her name, leaving for Nice, France, the very next day. She looked at the bracelet pensively. It had a style and a beauty from another age, with a patina that only came from time and wear. Perhaps, at some point in the past, the previous owner had also traced its smooth links with the tip of her fingers, just as she was doing now, while pondering over acts heavy with consequences. She took a deep breath, locked the bracelet on her wrist, and without thinking about it any further, called the concierge to arrange transportation for JFK the next day.

SHE SAT IN A CAR AS IT SPED AWAY from the buildings of Nice and made its way up a narrow road leaving the sea behind it. She kept the window open, taking in the sweet smells of the French countryside. The car seemed to glide by itself. Electric, she realized. It would take her a while to get used to the soundless engines, but that day it added another layer of wistfulness to the whole adventure. She did not know where she was going. She did not ask either. She did realize, as she was looking out dreamily through the window, that she missed Jim. Even Julie, she thought with a smile. A road sign indicated that they were close to the Fondation Maeght, the art museum in St. Paul de Vence.

The car made a sharp turn, continued up a short hill, slowed down, and then stopped. The driver opened the door for her and, without a word, pointed to the wooden doors at the entrance of a large mansion with walls made of earth-colored stone. Small windows punctuated its façade, like eyes looking at her.

Everything started to become a little daunting for Angelica. She felt the need to turn around and was about to ask the driver to take her back to Nice when the doors opened and an elderly woman with short gray hair and a sweet face came out to greet her. She was at once put to ease by the woman's aura. She seemed kind and gentle. Angelica smiled back. Until then, there had been no words exchanged, just impressions and shifts of movements. There were sounds to be heard, though, from the doves on the roof above to the bells ringing at a nearby church. Ten o'clock, she reckoned and, taking it as a good omen, followed the old woman into the house, her bracelet of gold like half a handcuff on her wrist.

Angelica quickly realized that the older woman only spoke French. With gestures and smiles, she made Angelica follow her into the back garden. The sun had just skimmed past the top of the tiled roof and lit up the white tablecloth draped over a rustic wooden table. A white umbrella shaded the breakfast spread laid out for her. There were bread and croissants, butter in a cup, and jam and honey in small jars. Only one seat, she noticed. She sat down at once, happy not to think too much and ready to accept it all as a gift, not a threat or a challenge. After all, she was the one who had decided to come.

She was still surprised at her own decision to accept the

"invitation." It had happened so fast and so unexpectedly. Somehow, the elegance of the gesture, the similar boxes, the golden jewelry, the sense of daring and adventure, all had appealed to her. She had nothing planned for the upcoming days, with her last modeling job completed and nothing more scheduled in New York for the next few months. She had been thinking about going to France even before being invited. Paris, really, but Nice was perfect too. She could take a quick flight to the capital whenever she wanted. All of this made it easy for her to go.

But mainly, she was intrigued. Who was this man who courted her with such attention? And mystery? And such panache! For one thing, he did not seem American, and she liked that. An American would have wanted an assurance of success before he sent such expensive gifts and would have revealed himself by now. Also, he would not have sent a vintage piece of jewelry. Americans believed in the new, like most people in the world. This was definitely European style, more likely Southern Europe, and with the ticket bound to Nice, it pointed to maybe a Frenchman. Hopefully tall! Well, he should be, judging from the size of that dildo he sent along with the string of pearls in the first box. Angelica's eyes twinkled at the memory. She recalled how that toy had felt deep in her the last time, and how that had become an added impetus for her to come.

A few other things had happened right after she opened

the second parcel too, and she was a believer in signs. "An angelic nod," her mother used to call them. First, there was the fact that the bracelet fit her so well, almost perfectly. Then, the magazine she was reading moments before she opened the blue box, had accidentally been left open on the coffee table with an aerial view of the Cote d' Azur, the seaside of the South of France. And then, when she looked out the window from her room at the Carlyle, she had witnessed her last sign: two red hawks flying close to the building, engaged in a circular dance that, in her current state of mind, could only mean one thing: "Go.Go!*GO!*"

TWO

NGELICA HAD BEEN RAISED to believe in herself. Both her parents trusted her and her opinions from an early stage. She allowed herself to make decisions, even hard ones, without looking back. She always had and it had served her right on most occasions. The ones that had turned out bad she did not look upon as failures but as stepping stones toward making the next one better. The important thing was to make the decisions. To commit to something.

In the breakfast garden, an ornate stone fountain was fed by a small clear spring. She could hear the water running, the hum of its flow gently filling her space. She let it fill her completely, as if living only for the secret connection between herself and the spring, enhanced by the faint buzz of an inquisitive dragonfly. She was content. She also felt fulfilled by the hot coffee, the lingering taste of the honey, and the wonderfully fresh French bread. Despite the jet lag, it was good to be alive. She always made sure to remember that.

Her mind at peace, she had been gazing into the deep emptiness when a large bird swooped down noiselessly and, in one motion grabbed the dragonfly. In the blink of an eye, the beautiful silvery-blue creature was gone. Angelica did not move. She kept breathing, working hard to maintain the same, even pace. She forced herself to. If this was another sign, an omen, she wanted to make sure she understood it as a vision of her being the bird seizing the moment rather than as the more ominous alternative. She turned her head around and looked at the wall behind her. That is when she noticed a remarkably tall magnolia growing along the side of the house. She could see its white flowers floating like small clouds amid the shiny green leaves. Everything was tranquil. The dragonfly was now a distant memory, the sound of the running water filling its absence. The chair she sat on, made squarely with solid wood, felt as if meant specifically for her to sit on, at this time, on this very occasion.

She stayed seated a while longer, emptying her thoughts and feeding on the abundance of nature so close to her. There were no thoughts of gold, or sex, or humans. Just of the slowly passing seconds that seemed to weigh more under the morning sun. And then, even that temporal notion of time vanished as fast as the dragonfly had disappeared, and she was left with an unexplainable feeling of bliss. Even for this moment alone, it would have been worth flying all the way here, she thought finally, as she heard the old woman approaching again.

"*Venez avec moi,*" said the woman. Come with me, understood Angelica, and she followed her into the three-story building. A small carved sign outside the entrance referred to it as a monastery for the Soeurs Dominicaines. It must have been a bustling monastery once, but for now it appeared entirely empty, except for the old woman and Angelica. They climbed to the top floor and Angelica was led to a vast room with two sets of windows overlooking the breakfast garden. "*Votre chambre,*" said the old woman. "*Celle que l'on reserve pour les invités d'honneur,*" she smiled. The room for special guests, Angelica, who could still remember a little high school French, could grasp. The woman pointed to her suitcases tucked in a cupboard. The driver must have brought them up, Angelica concluded. Then the woman showed her the bathroom attached to the room. It probably had been renovated recently, for it was luxurious without feeling out of sync with the monastic theme of the other rooms. The floor had smooth flat stones, and there were large white luminous tiles on all the walls.

The bathtub, though, was unexpected. It was red—a deep red. Like a cardinal! She smiled. The old woman was closing the shutters as Angelica came back into the bedroom. She then pulled the sheets back a little from the queen-sized bed and said, *"L'heure de dormir, Mademoiselle."*

Yes, time to sleep: Angelica realized how tired she was.

A narrow strip of light originating from the partially closed shutters illuminated the room's floor and the edge of her bed.

A narrow strip of light.

A narrow strip of her life.

She was going to live it the best way she knew how, without really thinking of all the consequences or clutter that come with thinking. But first, she was going to sleep. Later, she would assess the situation. A good thing they didn't do a luggage search; she smiled as she pulled the dildo out from her suitcase. There was no way she was going to sleep without an orgasm, and just then, there was no way she was going to have an orgasm without that dildo. She did not care for its pink color, but with eyes closed, she could focus on its size. Its girth filled her once again, right there, right on the spot. The fingers of her left hand did the rest, and she soon fell asleep, fast enough that she almost left the toy in her. She let it slip to the ground, its glistening surface capturing the edge of the light.

WHEN SHE WOKE UP, SHE NOTICED the ceiling with its original arches, painted all white like the rest of the room. Maybe this was a place of prayer in the past, she thought wistfully as she opened the shutters. The sun was still high in the sky and bathed her nudity with a kiss of early summer. Right outside her window, the magnolia tree had grown a white flower that had blossomed, displaying open petals and tender pistils right in front of her. Over the water fountain, a new dragonfly played again. They call them *libellule* in French, she remembered. A much more charming name, she thought.

Then she said to herself, as if whispering to her mom living continents away, "The angels are here!" She knew about angels. They were beings of light that conveyed emotional outputs in a loving, giving fashion. What they lacked in free will, they gained in empathy and brilliance. And she recognized them as they nudged the flower to bloom today and the libellule to hover once again over the water. They nudged nature to her favor, and she saw it for what it was—a miracle upon another miracle. Her legs were naked and spread open as she stood looking out the window. There was a faint knock on the door and then it slowly opened. She was tempted not to look, but she did. She turned her head around just enough to see the old woman enter the room with a tray of fruits and a green bottle of sparkling water. She did not move from the windowsill. She did not bring her legs together between the folds of her long white shirt. She did not move either when the old woman approached. She let her tie a ribbon over her eyes without a word. *"Restez ici,"* said the old woman, addressing her politely. Angelica did not disobey. And she did not move when the door closed and she heard two sets of footsteps, light ones leaving and much heavier ones coming closer. She kept her face to the sun, the flower who loved her, the flowing water, and all the birds. She did not move when the hands reached her hips and greeted her with a long slow, seductive caress, up the length of her spine and then her hair, over and over. She felt lips and kisses on her bare shoulder. Her shirt came undone. She moaned. It was a reflex as much as a response. It came from deep within her. It was a "yes," and it was a signal to bring her head further back.

He, for it was clearly a he from the touch of the hand and the rhythm of the breath, had also reacted to the moan. She could feel it. She moaned just a little more, and his hands went south. Her legs spread some more under his touch. Her hair was pulled back as hard as she had always wanted. His girth was as wide as she'd expected. A reunion of sorts. She smiled. She wanted it. She liked how hard she made him. She liked how fast he fucked her. She even liked the blindfold. She wanted to keep it on, almost as a precaution for herself, as if she was the one hiding from him. Then he came, all over her ass and lower back. She did not. She'd never intended to. She heard the door close behind her and was relieved to be alone in the room again, as if all that had happened was a summer storm that flowed right through her in the room. Like the libellule flying back and forth, and now back again. She took the blindfold off. She found the flower with her eyes. She sat down at the window, drank the water, and ate the fruit. She was fine with what had just happened. "He smelled good," she recalled. "And he tastes good, too."

Later in the evening, it happened again. The older woman walked in with a tray of food—salads and cheeses and wine. Before she walked out with the empty plates, she blindfolded Angelica again. And Angelica let her. As expected, he entered next.

She wanted that. There was a rhythm to it, a pendulum of expectations: silence–sex–food–repeat. She liked it that way, she thought.

This time, he faced her. He kissed her ever so gently as he touched her and found her wet. She wanted that too—to be wet for him. It was a gift, a sign that she was a participant. She was not thinking when she put her arms out in front of her. She kept her wrists together in a universal sign of acceptance. His belt tied tight around her arms, he attached her to the metal frame of the headboard. Her legs were pushed wide, and she let him dance between her moans. She tried keeping her sounds under as much control as she could, aware of the older woman and worried about what she would think. What would she think? It was not as if she had brought me volumes of Tolstoy to read with each meal! The bed made little noise, but it did amplify the speed at which he was moving. She loved the fast pace. It was just like what she had seen in the few porn videos she had watched. "Harder!" she told him. And he obliged, slamming his waist into hers with the full impact of animal lust. He did as she wanted but she did not cum, again. She already knew she wouldn't. He did, though, and with a final thrust he ejaculated all over her breasts. She smiled, knowing that soon she would be alone again and eat. She was getting hungry.

THREE

BREAKFAST WAS DOWN IN THE GARDEN again with very few words spoken, as usual. Time itself was starting to be transformed, as if things were moving around her rather than she moving among them. Lunch arrived, and with it the old woman carried garter belts for her to wear. They both laughed when the old woman noticed that Angelica was already wearing her own set. Hers were white; the ones the woman had brought were black. White is better for daytime, she decided, so she kept her own. In her mind, it was to be her final gift for now. She had had enough. And truth be told, she was getting sore and wanted to rest.

Angelica adjusted the garters, securing the straps and letting them hug all the right places yet support nothing. The beauty of such unnecessary luxury is just that—it is totally unneeded. That emptiness of function allows the mind to expand into it, like water filling up a vessel. She ran her fingers over the white garters, lifted a strap, and let it resound on her sloped hip. She wanted her image to arouse him, for that is what she is meant to do, and to make him cum fast, for she had already decided that this was to be the last time, at least in these circumstances.

He entered the room. He did not cum fast. On the contrary, he settled between the white straps, and with his mouth, spoke novels of love to her in a tongue she could understand.

She was there, almost there—and then he stopped. And before she could push his head back to where it belonged, he lifted her up and impaled her body on him. Sitting on top, she felt a rush travel through her, a spasm of pleasure that made her ride him like a horse. The white straps of the garters found a purpose now, as she moved like a participant at an equestrian competition. She bounced a few more times, biting her lips to keep the screams in, then leaned forward and he absolutely finished her with his constant motion. She came under his fingers, almost as soon as he placed his second finger up her ass. She pushed herself on it, allowing the gate to open. She held off tears, ever so close to removing the blindfold, and found his lips. She kissed him with tenderness and the passion closest to love, revealing herself to him for the very first time.

FOUR

HE LEFT HER AS USUAL, but this time he had stayed a while longer after they were done with the torrential sex. He stayed by her, caressing her shoulders and the small of her back with soft slow strokes of his right hand. She liked that, and she nestled a little closer to him, her nose in his neck, inhaling his masculine scent, breathing it in with each rise of his chest.

Then he kissed her forehead, got up, and left. She fell asleep almost instantly, the jet lag still lingering. It was only later, after she took a bath with salts in that crazy red bathtub, that she realized that although she had reached the clouds this morning, he had not cum. And she kind of liked that, the fact that it was not about his pleasure only. But also she somehow felt bad about it. As if she had failed. She tilted her head backward, plunging herself underwater, and blew bubbles through her nose. By the time she got out again, all sense of failure had been flushed away.

Outside, rapidly moving gray clouds darkened the sky. In the incoming wind, the leaves in the trees revealed their undersurface, a paler shade of green that trembled and waved, a gift to whoever was watching.

A storm was coming.

She wrapped her hair in one of the luxurious towels that had been left for her in the bathroom, and she sat on a small wooden stool by the open window. She could feel the storm building strength from a distance. She could almost smell it. She could hear it.

The first drops landed heavily on the ground. She saw them pierce the veil of green water in the fountain. They matched her tears, falling heavily as well, darkening the pale stone floor. She felt no real sadness, though, only alone and a little lost. Her mom did not really exist any longer, and Dad was long gone. She thought of him as she looked at the rainfall, remembering how it had not stopped him from doing anything in the past. Her dad had gone out for a run in the pouring rain once, she recalled, and he had told her, "It only makes you stronger," as he walked out.

Soon the tears were gone. She was over whatever it had been that submerged her. As if she had needed these tears as a complement to her morning pleasure.

What on earth am I doing? she wondered again. It was one thing to let yourself float on the currents of destiny and happenstance, another to drift away with no anchor and no horizon in sight. All her life she had felt different from others. She "acted" her life, and maybe she had not lived it. But then again, she portrayed it with an inner impulse that came from somewhere deep in her, a force that drove her, even compelled her, to do certain things. It empowered her to leave her home early and rely on her looks to hone the skills she needed to navigate life. She soon discovered that the world is one of action, where the material prevailed. And so, she used the materiality of her own body, her beautiful body, in order to extract the lessons she needed to learn and the spirituality that she ultimately sought.

She had no phone service in her room and, by default, lived in meditative silence, interrupted only by sex and food, and food and sex. She had watched the magnolia flower grow and blossom, feed insects and bees, and then die, all in the span of the last two days. She had sat by the window and waited for things to unfold, within her as well maybe—for things to blossom and maybe even die. She had not waited for the sex, but she did not mind its arrival either. It was intimate and mysterious all at once. It brought with it a palpable affirmation of her existence and its own taste of fragility. She let it all happen, almost as a delusion, for somewhere deep in her psyche she did acknowledge the fact that she might know who the visitor was.

The storm switched her reverie. She had seen the rain come down in literal sheets of water, sheets she could almost pull and wrap around her shoulders like a magical garment. The raindrops bounced thick and heavy, almost as if intentionally, on the stone sill of her open window. She had let the splashes reach her, feeling the coolness of the rainwater on her naked legs, and watched her skin get wet, bit by bit, making her legs luminous when the gray in the sky vanished under the wind and sun. She did not move. She kept her legs stretched out in front of her, reached for her phone, and took a picture of them. She could see the small dimples of cold raised up along their length. Lit by the returning sun, her wet skin glistened like gold against the open frame of the window and the leaves of the magnolia tree beside it. The fragrant flower was now completely gone, blown away by the raging storm. She knew it was time to move on, and she knew exactly what she wanted to do as she looked at the image a little longer.

FIVE

THE DOOR TO HER ROOM HAD NEVER been locked, she just lacked the desire to move out of it or keep anyone else out. She had liked it that way. She watched the day pass from her bed, or the seat by the window, or the depths of the red bathtub. She had been, as she termed it, "actively passive," trying to receive. And she had received. Of all she had been given, the tomatoes, red and delicious, were her favorite. Those as well as his cock, so plentiful and muscular in the darkness of the blindfold. But now she was ready to leave.

Without hesitation, she opened the door and walked past the same succession of dark rooms that she had followed on the way in. The sweet smell of old furniture followed her all along. The old woman must wax them, she thought as she let a hand glide over a smooth console. Maybe she was a nun here once. A strange thought, considering the role she had been playing nowadays. But she did fit in with this house, and maybe she also did whatever it took to keep it afloat. And the blindfolding, hm. . . . Perhaps a nod to the sacrificial lamb? She smiled as she finally left the house from the front door. She hurried down the path that led to the small road where the car had driven her. She did not want anyone to call her back. She walked faster, unaware that the old woman, who was working in her vegetable garden, saw her walk by and smiled under her wide-brimmed hat.

Angelica made her way down a small side street, past the shadow of the house she had just left, and along other large private homes before reaching the village of St. Paul de Vence. She noticed the first door that was open and saw it as an invitation. An omen. And it was a fantastic one. She had just walked into the fabulous La Colombe d'Or Hotel and, "Yes, we do have a room for you," they said. A party of two rooms had just cancelled minutes ago. She could choose whichever she wanted. They were both free for a week. And yes, they would go and pick up her luggage from the old monastery. They knew it and they knew the old lady.

She had settled in the room of her choice, on the first floor above the swimming pool, when she had a sudden realization and rushed back to the reception desk. "I'll take both rooms for the week," she told the receptionist, who did not bat an eye.

It was five in the morning when Julie's phone pinged. She did not mind. She was up already, resting in bed, working on separating her mind from her body—not an easy task, and one best tried in the earliest hours of the morning, before reality weighed in. It was never clear to her if she was imagining the out-of-body experiences or if they were really happening. Nevertheless, she kept trying, mindful of Guillaume d'Orange's saying: "*Il n'est pas nécessaire d'espérer pour entreprendre ni de réussir pour persévérer*," which translated in English as "There is no need to hope in order to undertake, nor to succeed in order to persevere."

The phone call interrupted her effort, but the message was worth the disruption. It was even worth calling, and certainly waking up, Jim. She could not resist. As soon as he picked up and answered with a voice full of lost sleep, she told him, "Pack your bags. We're going on a trip!"

"Where?" muttered the suddenly awakened voice.

"South of France. We are shooting Angelica. We leave today!" she exclaimed.

"OK!" he said, not missing a beat. "I'm psyched!"

Julie upgraded them both to business class when they got to the airport, and for the first time in his life, Jim turned left as he boarded the plane. He was so excited he almost jumped over the partition to kiss Julie. She asked him if he was OK with sharing a room once they got to the hotel. He beamed and became even more excited, drinking the welcome-to-the-flight champagne in one gulp.

It was a long flight and he found sleep as soon as he laid his long frame down on the stretched-out seat, but not before he found her scent with the tip of his long fingers.

They arrived at the hotel just in time for lunch. They left their bags in their room with its own small terrace facing the swimming pool. Julie marveled at the lushness of the plants all around it, with the green of nature reflecting itself even deeper in the water. She pointed out to him the marvel of a full blooming magnolia flower right at the edge of their terrace and a bee sucking on it in the hot noon sun. "That's what I want to do to you," he commented. "That and much more, I hope." She replied with a smile and a wink. He pulled her closer to him. He had changed to a pair of fancy swimming trunks from a past fashion shoot and, through the smooth fabric, she could feel that he meant business. "Not now," she said. "Angelica is expecting us."

"Now! Fast," he said as he pushed her back into the room and onto the edge of the bed, lifting up the short skirt she wore and pushing aside her phone. She felt his lips moving on her, his teeth biting the fleshy part of her ass and shifting towards the middle. "No!" she said, "I haven't even had time for a shower yet."

"That's the way I like it," he replied as he pushed her flat on the bed, moving her underwear aside in one motion. And there, he feasted on his first meal. She closed her eyes and bit her lips, keeping within her the moans that were building stronger and stronger as she felt the fullness of his being find its way into her. She tasted herself on his lips as he found hers, and they both came at the same time, rushing their linked pleasures before sitting down like good guests at Angelica's lunch table.

The white wine soon mixed itself with the carnal taste that lingered within. "You look rested," Angelica said with a knowing smile.

She looked beautiful, thought Julie, looking up at the large white umbrella over them and noticing how soft Angelica's features were under the filtered light. They shared a fish cooked ever so perfectly, the white flesh detaching itself in delicious flakes and redolent of the sea with each bite.

A very fishy affair, thought Jim, and he smiled so broadly that Angelica had to ask why. "Oh, it's just the pleasure of being here right now. Eating this beautiful food, drinking chilled wine with two incredibly beautiful women. Lots to smile about," he added, and he looked deep into Julie's eyes.

"Tell us, what brought us here?" Julie asked Angelica. Jim, seated across from them, saw a man enter the restaurant, take a few steps, and turn around as soon as he spotted their table. He became aware of the man's presence, as he was of all things around him, but he did not pay special attention to him. Instead, he turned his attention back to Angelica, eager to hear her response as well.

"Well, it's an odd story," she replied, and she began to explain how the man who had given her the dildo and pearl necklace had invited her there. And she told them, as she would old friends, what had happened since her arrival.

She told them everything. It was cathartic. The wine freed her tongue, and their attentive silence engaged her to talk even more and divulge all. She spoke for them as much as she spoke for herself, astonished at her own words, at her own description of what had happened, and was filled with an inexplicable mélange of pride and shame. She looked up at Julie when she was done, the shadow of a question in her eyes.

"It's alright," said Julie. "You did what your sense of adventure told you to, and once you'd lived it, you took matters in your own hands. . . . And," she added with a smile, "that bracelet fits you very well."

Angelica looked at it. She had almost forgotten it. It fit just too well. She smiled back. "You noticed?"

"Yes," Julie replied. "It has a very particular presence. Kudos to whoever bought it."

"That was him again," said Angelica.

"I thought so," chuckled Julie. "He has good taste. And it seems like a good fit, too!"

They all laughed as a selection of desserts was brought to the table. "We didn't order dessert yet," said Jim.

The waiter answered, "A gentleman ordered it for the table, sir."

It all started to make sense to Jim. He was not sure if Angelica, accustomed to receiving favors and attention from strangers, got it yet.

She looked around the room. There were no single men, only full tables. No one looked at her with a raised glass in hand. She stopped searching and kept talking with Julie. She told them she wanted to start shooting that day. She wanted various pictures at various times of day and in various states of undress, right by the giant Calder sculpture that bordered the small edge of the pool. Julie could even shoot her from above, if she wanted, from the balcony of her first-floor room.

"Would that not be the second floor?" Jim asked.

"Not in Europe," said Angelica. "Here, they count the ground floor zero."

"Hm," he said. "That could explain why we're so often out of sync!" They cheered again and clinked their wine glasses over the almond tarte and tiramisu.

"I can't tell you how excited I am to be here," he said to Angelica. "Thank goodness you're such an adventurous person."

"You mean such a slut!" she laughed, and they cheered again as if there was no tomorrow—for who knew? Maybe there wasn't.

SIX

THEY STARTED WORKING, IF YOU could call it work, after lunch. Angelica had another bottle of white wine brought to the pool. There, they were shaded by a dense, bushy tree, and they were pretty much alone that time, yet they could feel eyes looking at the pool and at them, eyes from other rooms and from occasional guests walking in from the restaurant. They did not mind. Julie had Angelica do laps in the pool first to capture the essence of the daylight. She swam beautifully, with slow strokes that made her glide in the water almost without a splash. Julie followed her with the lens and found the drops of water streaming from a raised hand at each stroke so mesmerizing that she started shooting right away. Angelica was unaware that they had started, and when she flipped onto her back and shifted to a backstroke,

Julie found the perfect shot—with arms raised toward sculpture, Angelica's breasts floated at the surface of the shimmering water, and her smile of utter satisfaction was lost between thin, translucent layers of water. It was almost like a scene from the movies in the '50s when swimmers glided on the silver screen, glamorous and romantic.

They shot more pictures while slowly sipping the wine kept cool in an ice bucket by the chairs. Jim was taking pictures from a different angle, but at one point he got into the pool, sat Angelica on his shoulders, and with her thighs hanging from each side of his neck, raised her out of the water. He could feel her on his nape, pressed softly against him. He said nothing. He tried nothing. He was here for Julie and no one else, with that moment in the bathroom at the Carlyle being just that—a moment that was now gone with time and space. Angelica felt him too, felt his thick neck between her legs and laughed at it, and it made the pictures that much better. The sex, or at least the idea of sex, filled up all the empty space on the image. She looked radiant, almost like an Amazon riding her steer, the white bathing suit tight against her figure.

Julie sat in the shaded area, waiting for that magical instant, as on a safari trip when the animal will play to your wishes and eventually reveal itself in shades and light for your pleasure. She took a shot of Angelica as she laughed while riding Jim, who was ever so kind. "Maybe too kind," she murmured, and her lips tightened just a bit as she reevaluated her next shot. But then again, this was not any ordinary woman. It was Angelica, a mysterious creature capable of opening up things in the universe. Julie shook her head and let out a slow breath. Then she saw Angelica remove her bathing suit top and wrap it around Jim's eyes placing one white cup, like a patch, on each eye: a play on her own blindfolding. A play on life. Julie couldn't help but laugh.

A LITTLE WHILE LATER, ANGELICA, AS EXCITED as she was to know that Julie and Jim were there with her, felt suddenly strangely lonely in her beautiful room, with her beautiful naked body lying on perfect sheets and no one to see it. She thought about calling them again to take more pictures of her but decided not to. They were surely exhausted from traveling and, knowing Jim, they probably were making love.

And they were, lying side by side as lovers do. He in her, legs wrapped around each other, his hand touching her ever so softly, almost like a lullaby of sex, in a slow, gentle rocking motion.

"How did she feel around your neck?" she asked suddenly.

"Who?" he answered.

"Come on, you know who!" she exclaimed. "I'm not upset," she added calmly. "I actually enjoyed watching her wrapped around you."

He remembered how she had shown him another side of her not that long ago, with the wife from the luxury Upper

East Side townhouse. He relaxed some more, and he started to talk to her and tell her all the things he would do to her. He let his words find their way between the intensity of her moans until he needed no words anymore and she climaxed again next to him. Before she could drift away, he got up on his knees and lifted her up in front of him, taking her without pity. One hand clenched her hair, suddenly astonishingly long, and the other slapped her to another peak in another valley.

They slept—not too long to get groggy and not function any longer, but long enough to feel refreshed and ready for coffee and a walk. They walked out of the hotel, past the central square where the locals were playing Pétanque. The players were throwing heavy metal balls towards a smaller wooden one they called the cochonnet. An English tourist took the time to explain the rules to them. Cochonnet, "a little pig," Julie remembered from her French classes. The players were mainly men, and they played with such intensity that, even though Jim did not quite understand all the rules, he stayed for a while, fascinated. All activities done with passion were worth enjoying, he knew by then. Behind the players, he recognized the man from the hotel making a sharp left turn up a hill. He was the same one who stared at them during lunch. Again, Jim decided to ignore him.

He left the game and walked up the hills of the small village with Julie. Like most mountaintop-fortified villages, it had kept a medieval feel. But where there had once been cobblers and butchers and maybe even a forge, there was now a gallery and a store full of postcards and trinkets. Where people had once lived and roamed now were paths where tourists walked, slipping on the slippery centennial stones.

Julie took off her shoes and walked barefoot. Jim marveled at her one more time. She had so many ways of being sexy. To him. To his growing love. She stepped on small, rounded stones clustered together like flowers. He remembered the magnolia flowers back in their room. "Let's go back to the hotel," he urged her. She did not disobey.

SEVEN

LE COCHONNET. HE THOUGHT ABOUT that little piggy again at the center of all the metal balls that landed around it like heavy rain. "Might as well call it a little pussy!" he laughed to himself.

"What is it?" asked Julie.

"Nothing, darling," he said, and then he caught himself. That was the first time he had called her that. She also noted it, for she stopped whatever unpacking she was doing in the room and turned to look at him. "Yes," he repeated, "Darling." And she came close to him and melted in his arms.

THEY WERE GOING TO SHOOT AGAIN after dinner, so they planned for an early meal. Early there meant 8:30 p.m., and Jim was astonished. He was starving already. How did they manage? he wondered, staring at the drink in front of him, wishing it was actual food instead. Cocktail hour came with the prerequisite local drink. It was a yellow, licorice-tasting liqueur called Pastis that turned a beautiful shade of white when poured over ice and made time go faster. After one drink, they were all in a very jovial mood, and they started the second one with much more laughter and lightness. The saltiness of the crispy chips made them thirstier, and the drinks made them hungrier. They were caught in a delightful loop of self-fulfilling pleasure, far away from the grid of Manhattan, the asphalt, and the fast-moving cars and taxis.

All around them, paintings from a bygone era hung on the restaurant walls—Picasso, Braque, Dufy, Léger, and others, silent beacons of thought and taste and achievement. "I have something to say," said Angelica.

Julie and Jim went silent. She was standing by a black-and-white photograph of Picasso as she spoke, and it almost seemed as if he too was listening.

"I received a note today. From the guy. From my mysterious man. My mysterious lover, I should say. He says he wants to meet with me later tonight in my room. And that I should decide if I want that or not. And whether I want to remain blindfolded or not."

"How would you recognize him?" Jim asked.

"No scarf tied to my balcony means no go. A white one means yes. A red one, yes, blindfolded."

"And I gather he forwarded the appropriate scarves to your room?" asked Julie.

"Yes. How did you guess? Beautiful scarves, in fact. The softest silk I've ever felt.".

They were all silent for a while. "So what are you going to do?" asked Jim.

"I don't know yet," she said, looking at Julie, who smiled.

"The red scarf for sure," said Julie as she got up to walk to their table. "We should eat now. We have work to do!" she added as they all smiled different smiles.

EIGHT

THE MAÎTRE D' SAT THEM at a round table right by the entrance of the hotel. From there, you could see everybody, and everyone could see you. And they were truly a beautiful sight to behold. Jim had dressed up—a thin white cotton shirt, dark blue pants, and the dusty pink espadrilles he bought in the village earlier in the day. Angelica was in a long red cotton dress. She'd had a tailor cinch it even closer to her body, around her belly and waist, like a bodice. Her breasts were elegantly buoyant, revealing the string of pearls that shone bright along her still winter-pale skin. The bottom of the dress flowed with her steps as she walked. Jim smiled as he noticed her playing absent-mindedly with the string of pearls, caressing them like beads of a rosary.

Julie was in a saffron linen dress that blended with the

softly tanned skin she had acquired from running outdoors. It showed off her arms, which moved gracefully as she spoke and highlighted her neckline, adorned by a simple gold chain necklace. She was touching her necklace, too—a gift from Henry a long time ago.

It was a long, long time ago. Back when Henry was full of life and vigor. She remembered him taking her over and over in their hotel room. Actually, at one point, in this very hotel, and in the same room that she now shared with Jim. She still could not believe it. The whole thing was just too incredible to fathom, and so she had not told Jim. Instead, she kept looking up at the three little cross-shaped voids in the ceiling above the bed as he took her—the same three voids she had looked at when Henry took her on the same bed. And tonight, the lovely chain hung around her neck for her sake as much as for Henry's: a sign for him to know that he was here with her and at all times. Even when she was having fun eating at a table where they used to share their own meals or having fun with Jim's eager mouth eating her out in their old room. Even then. Even when Jim was in her, looking at her radiant face and the faint glitter of the golden chain around her neck, unaware of what she was thinking. Even when she agreed to do everything he asked as he whispered words of decadent passion in her ears. In case he was looking down from his perch in the afterlife.

They ordered the same fish dish they'd had at lunch. The

bottle they had not finished by the pool was already waiting for them in a translucent ice bucket. The white wine shimmered through layers of glass and ice like a secret elixir. The meal was wonderful. Julie ordered the soufflé for dessert. When it arrived, the waiter poured Calvados on it and lit it ablaze. Blue and yellow flames leaped from the plate. It was a moment of pure exalted joy for the three of them, of being kids again with laughter, candy, and surprises. The simple kind. Not the ones that were about to unfold.

INITIALLY THE PLAN HAD BEEN TO GET naked pictures of Angelica in the dark, evanescent water of the swimming pool after dinner, but somehow the mood for nude photos was not there. And Angelica didn't want to get her hair wet again, in case she was going to see her guest. And who was she kidding? Of course, she was going to have him tonight! Just as Julie had said. Her inner debate had shifted to the color of scarf she was to use. Red or white?

Instead, they took pictures of her standing by the Calder sculpture, which was mesmerizing. Centered on a solid black metal base, two long arms with cut-out shapes in various colors moved freely. The most striking shapes were the three red ones, and, standing next to the sculpture in her red dress, Angelica looked absolutely stunning. You could see on the camera screen the opulence of that moment, Angelica and the sculpture complementing each other rather than fighting for supremacy. Even Calder would have liked it, thought Julie, who had seen her share of his work over the years. She was not satisfied with the shoot, though. It was all too predictable, too organized, too perfect. Then, in a flash, she saw what had to happen and went to Angelica to ask her to do one last thing.

The red dress was splayed open in a wide circle around Angelica as she stood in the pool, her legs an echo of light under the surface and her hair, pulled in a bun, still dry. Her lips were deep red with the added lipstick, and her pale pink nipples hovered just above the line of the décolleté. Julie moved the arms of the sculpture one last time so that the panels of color could find their right place and she started shooting from the side of the pool. Jim, understanding Julie's vision, quickly slipped into the water to take his own shots from inside the pool. They moved fast, wanting to get their pictures before other guests arrived.

It was all worth it. The final shots looked great. Julie was pleased, and Jim jumped out buck naked to help Angelica out of the pool. Just then, an elderly couple walked past them, nodding in approval, as if agreeing to the display of blatant nudity and explosion of colors. What else did you expect in an artist's refuge?

NINE

THE ELDERLY COUPLE WAS CERTAINLY fast asleep by the time she decided to tie the scarf on the balcony railing. It was still light enough outside for the color to make an imprint in the surrounding air, as if a flag—not of surrender but of crimson carnal intent.

Angelica was in the bathroom fixing her hair up when she heard a faint knock at the door. She thought it was Julie bringing something over, but to her surprise, it was the older woman from the monastery. She stared at the bowl of food in her hands. "*Je n'ai pas faim,*" she said with a smile, because she wasn't hungry.

"*Ce sera pour après,*" the woman answered. Ah, for after: Angelica offered a polite smile as she let the woman set the food down. With it was a wooden bowl with Angelica's favorite tomatoes, plump and ripe and deliciously red. They matched her underwear, and it seemed, her new blindfold. The woman came closer with a wide strip of thick red satin, and the girl let herself be blindfolded, wondering why it was that she felt compelled to do this over and over again. She told herself that tonight would be the absolute last. She was completely taken by surprise, though, when the woman told her, *"Laissez-moi faire,"* and, taking her by the hand, guided her to the bed. The old woman positioned her spread-eagle on the sheets, face-down, and proceeded to tie her limbs to the four corners of the bed frame. Satin straps, thought Angelica, and if she knew her man by now, most likely red. She had been tied before, by earlier lovers in previous iterations, though very rarely. And never face down. Somehow, she liked it. Face-down gave her a feeling of deferential submission and, after all, was this not what this game was about? It was all a game, just as her life was all an act. For now, she wanted this, this novel sensation, and she also wanted the waiting time, which began as soon as she heard the woman gather her things and step away.

The solid thump of the closing door left her completely alone. "Oh! Did I fall asleep?" she exclaimed when she heard the door open again. She could smell him before she could hear him or feel his touch. She loved his smell, and that alone made all of it possible. He caressed her at first, tracing with his long fingers the curves of her bound body, the same way she had touched the marble Miro sculptures at the Maeght Foundation earlier that day. She knew his fingers. She knew how long they were and how high they reached in her, and she knew that today they would probe her even further. She knew it the same way you could feel a storm coming even before the sky turns entirely dark gray. She spread her legs wider apart for him. The underwear she had picked was in itself an invitation, the red garment conveniently designed with no fabric in the back. He uncovered her, revealed her, and led himself, one finger at a time, into voids so full of taboos that both of them breathed heavily in anticipation. Their combined breaths, and the melodic sound of a lone night swimmer in the pool below them, were the only sounds that could be heard. She knew he could not slap her without catching attention. She held her breath as he took her cheeks between his hands and squeezed her hard before biting them, teeth deep in her, tongue searching her even deeper.

And she moaned. It was a muffled sound, with her face in the pillow. She felt the weight of his naked body against hers and his rigid manhood sliding up and down the valley of her ass, lathered by his saliva. "Take me," she said. And then she said again, "Take me, please."

He did not disobey, and not long after he was riding her, gently at first, and then faster when her body fully adapted to him. He rode in a slow rhythm that somehow seemed to match the strokes of the swimmer in the pool outside. Going back and forth. In and out. He was spreading her cheeks for her, biting the nape of her neck, inserting his fingers in her mouth, and then riding her faster, letting the hips move at their own rhythm, their own volition.

Outside, the swimmer paused his routine, thinking he had heard a scream. He looked around but all was quiet. He resumed his laps from one end to the other.

Angelica buried her face deep in the pillow and let her body quiver with undeniable pleasure. When she felt him cum in deep long throbs, she turned her face to the side and said with a smile, "You really had me there."

He laughed. A deep, beautiful, manly laugh she realized she had never heard before. She liked him even more after she heard it and laughed with him as he rested his head, still panting, beside hers on the pillow. That is when he slowly released her arms from the satin ribbons. Her wrists were sore, she realized, from pulling against the ribbons as she was being invaded and taken. She put her arms around him and felt his breath on her as they kissed tenderly, surrounded only by the scent of the sex they'd had and the sounds of the final laps of the swimmer. Soon they heard him get out of the pool and walk away.

The moonlight was shining brightly into the room, bouncing off the panes of the open windows. He could see it being captured in the thick white pearls oozing out of her, framed in red silk. The sight was an echo to the sculpture outside—a moving, living Calder sculpture. He finished untying her legs and leaned over to kiss her as she said, "If there is to be a next time, I want to see you. No more blindfolds."

She heard him leave, shutting the door behind him. She kept the blindfold on for just a few more moments, savoring the stillness that came with it. As she slipped it down her face, she saw how bright the moon had become, like a silver sun. Great light to take pictures, she thought, and without hesitation she texted Julie, *You up?*

Yes, Julie replied. *Jim just came back from his swim.*

Can you shoot me quickly? Angelica smiled at her message, amused at how she sounded almost like a junkie. *The light is great in the room now and my blindfold is off. . . .*

Coming over, Julie replied.

Come alone.

I was planning to.

Angelica was suddenly hungry for a ripe tomato. She was reaching for one from the wooden bowl when Julie entered the room and thought, My goodness, she looks incredible!

The girl's face was aglow with the fruit of orgasm, and the red blindfold she wore loosely around her neck spoke of her power and subjugation. Behind her the unraveled red ribbons, which moments ago had kept her tied down, were lying quietly like forgotten snakes on the white sheets.

Julie started shooting just as Angelica took a bite of the plump tomato, spilling its contents all over her chin and chest.

It trickled down to her breasts, still strapped in a red lace bal-conette. Angelica was about to wipe the spill with a clean nap-kin when Julie said, "No, leave it like that," and kept shooting. She captured the eyes, wide from the recent action, and the lips, swollen from being bitten to be quiet. She took pictures of the red juices that slipped down Angelica's skin from her chin to her breasts, like a vestige of a past encounter. Julie wanted more of it, and she asked Angelica to bite into more fruits. With each bite, she let more of the warm, ripe flesh flow down, slowly lathering her up, as if creating an organic exten-sion of the red choker she was wearing so casually around her neck—as if it was the creation of some extraordinary fashion designer, maybe Alexander McQueen. . .or maybe just the fingers of fate.

Angelica was a natural model. She did not mind keeping the same pose for a while, and she could will her emotions to the surface of her skin, of her face. Julie loved that. She could find the angles she wanted, and she could take fewer pictures, making the ones she took more relevant. Or at least bring as much relevance as one could to photos like these.

Yet taking relevant photos was not Julie's sole focus just then. On her screen, she watched Angelica naked, sitting nude on a towel spread over the chair. In a soft but firm voice, she told her to go lie back on the bed. Angelica did so. "No, face up," Julie ordered, and the girl shifted, her body moist and vi-brating initially under the lens, and then under Julie's tongue as Julie lowered herself onto her and first licked the juices of the squashed tomatoes that had dripped down to Angelica's thighs and then the wetness of her open pussy, all pungent from the recent sex and penetration. Julie brought her to the crest and when her fingers traveled higher, Angelica's eyes rolled back, her toes curled in, and her voice finally let out a slow, tender moan that spoke directly to the solitary owl outside.

AFTER LEAVING ANGELICA'S ROOM, JULIE STOOD for a while on the landing facing the swimming pool. All was quiet and sublime. There was a gentle song in the tree that told her of the owl hiding in the branches. Across the pool, she noticed the outline of a human figure standing by a window. It was late for anyone to be up at that time. She smiled.

Jim was asleep by the time she got back to bed with him. She loved spreading the length of her body against his, feeling his mass and his breath as she got even closer to him.

He woke from his deep sleep and, without missing a beat, wrapped his arms around her. In a very quiet voice, he told her, "I just had the weirdest dream. You and Angelica were at lunch together and all you ordered was a plate of tomatoes. And then you both bit on the same one. The juices and seeds were all over your faces. It was strange."

Julie smiled and brought her lips closer to his. He was still half asleep but must have recognized the scent on her mouth, for moments later he was all strength and vitality as he found her over and over before they both fell back to sleep together.

"What happened last night?" he asked when they woke up the next morning.

"I will tell you all about it later, cowboy," Julie said. "First, kiss me good morning."

He did. They linked in the narrow beam of light that had somehow found its way between the overlapping bedroom curtains.

TEN

JULIE MET ANGELICA AT THE BREAKFAST TABLE on the dining terrace. It was beautiful in the early morning sun. There were very few people up, only hotel guests and no outsiders. The hotel was like a huge home, with guests navigating the place as if it were their own. Jim was doing early morning laps in the pool.

They sat close to the entrance under the shade of a leafy tree and faced an incredible ceramic mural by Fernand Léger. It was an explosion of women and flowers and had a large bird that looked as it could fly out at any moment. The mural had an overwhelming presence, like an image in a movie screen about to come to life.

Julie realized how much of her life had the same cinematic quality, as if she was moving from one scene to the next, and how she did not really mind it at all. It might all be fluff, she reflected, but at least it brought pleasure and sensations.

Maybe that was better than what her other realities could offer. Maybe it was her life's consequences. On a trip she made to Tulum, a shaman had once approached her unexpectedly and told her, "There are no coincidences, only consequences." Maybe she was there because of Angelica. Or maybe it was just part of her destiny, ascending upward effortlessly, like a feather floating in the air against gravity. Whatever it might be, she had decided to accept it. She was happy; she could feel it. It was a full life. She knew Henry would approve.

"Well, listen to this," said Angelica. "I received a text message this morning from Helena—you remember, the one I introduced to Alexander? Well, she's coming to La Colombe d'Or tonight."

"You mean the Alexander who picked you out from the three women we photographed a while back?"

"Yes, that Alexander. I posted a picture of the pool here with the Calder, and Helena texted me right away that she was also coming."

"What does this mean?" asked Julie. "Is this a coincidence or something else?"

"I think that the secret guy is Alexander himself," replied Angelica. "It kind of makes sense now, and I thought I recognized his scent when I first met him. Well, not really met since

I could not see who it was. . . .."

"Well, I believe I know where he may be staying," said Julie as she explained how she had seen a window lit late the previous night with someone clearly behind it.

"So that's how he saw my red scarf hanging from the balcony!" said Angelica. "And now Helena will be here, most likely with him, together in that room. Maybe I should tell her? Warn her?"

"You will do nothing of the sort," Julie said firmly. "Surely you don't know all this to be true. And even if it was, you don't know what they're all about. Just wait and see."

Jim ambled up to the table and joined them. He had a towel wrapped around his waist and a loosely buttoned shirt over his shoulders. They seemed even broader to Julie in the morning light. She smiled at the faint imprint the goggles had left around his eyes. Like a fake superhero mask. She smiled again thinking to herself, Is he naked under the towel?

The girls said nothing more about Helena or Alexander. They ate their breakfast and talked about plans for the day. Julie suggested they all go together to Antibes by the coast, see the Picasso Museum there, and then have lunch at the Eden-Roc restaurant at Hotel du Cap. She had stayed there once with Henry, long ago, and still remembered the great pool that seemed to melt into the nearby sea. Angelica liked the idea. She was ready for a change of pace. They decided to meet again in an hour.

Jim was stoked. New places. New faces. New spots to swim in. He told the front desk to get their car ready. He looked forward to driving. He had driven tractors as a kid and was probably one of the few left in the U.S. who could still drive stick. He went back to their room, giddy with excitement.

JULIE WAS WAITING FOR HIM. She was wearing short running shorts and a jogging bra, prepared to go on a quick run. She was sitting on the edge of their bed, socks in hand, and had a big smile on her face when he walked in.

"Tell me, cowboy," she said, "are you wearing anything under that towel?"

"Well, now, li'l lady," he teased, "that is for me to know, and for you to find out."

He took three steps forward and stopped right beside her. Her skin was hot with anticipation, but she did not blush.

It was actually quite fun, she thought. She felt younger around Jim, sexier, more alive. And even though she didn't consider it a true, serious, long-standing relationship, she was happy to be aboard that ship. After all, there she was in a magical place in the South of France, about to unravel this hunk of a guy's towel and surely discover more bliss.

The sun shone through the small windowpanes. It had traveled along the same walls in a quiet way long ago. Oblivious to who the lovers were, the sunlight fulfilled its sole mission, blasting itself all over the world for the ones free enough to see it.

Jim was indeed free under the dark blue towel and on him she could faintly taste the pool. She buried her head further under the towel until they were linked by flesh and fabric like a centaur soon to reshape itself. Jim lifted her up in the air and then laid her back on their unmade bed, his naked body on her. She took her shorts off.

"Fuck the run," she said laughingly.

"No, fuck the runner."

Daytime sex has the peculiarity that it is not anchored to sleep. There is no other desire to perhaps let go and fall asleep if it occurs in the evening, nor is there any of the residual sleepiness that accompanies early morning lovemaking. Laziness cannot flavor the daytime experience. No, during daytime, sex becomes a deliberate choice. A decision to lie back in bed and engage in each other. Or not in bed, perhaps standing, or kneeling. Her eyes were wide open as she looked at Jim's arms lodged like two columns on either side of her. She let her fingers run on them, on his back, on the top of his ass. She let her hands travel to places that she could barely reach until he came lower to her, and she could grab him and impose her rhythm on him.

ELEVEN

I N HER ROOM, ANGELICA HAD HER EYES CLOSED. She'd blindfolded herself with the red scarf and was sitting on the chair facing the window Julie had pointed to earlier. She had one leg up on the desk next to her. She was naked except for an unbuttoned shirt she'd borrowed from Jim the day before. She knew that was a look that made her even more desirable. She wanted him, Alexander or whoever it was, to be mesmerized, enthralled even. She knew that soon she would not be able to expose herself, fearful of Helena's presence. Her fingers found her body and displayed it to the sky, and perhaps his gaze. Perhaps to someone else's gaze too, she realized, noting the number of windows facing her. But she didn't care. And the blindfold helped. She didn't need to see to reach the destination she was seeking. She moved the fabric aside and moaned very quietly. There were people already by the side of the pool below her, lounging on beach chairs and chaises and towels, reading books by themselves or whispering to each other, unaware of what was happening beyond the first balcony—so close to each other yet worlds apart. She was in her own world by then—a world she had created moment after strong moment. She had made a choice, long ago, and the usual lifestyle with its rules and regulations just wasn't for her. She wanted freedom—first and foremost, freedom to do as she pleased, and freedom to suffer the consequences, whatever they might be.

She remembered walking in a forest at the footsteps of mountains in upstate New York with her father. They'd reach a ridge and travel down into another small valley, and then do it again over the next ridge, until they could hear no cars anymore and only the sound of woodpeckers could break the silence. She had loved those walks, seemingly getting lost, except that her dad always knew where they were and, before she knew it, they would be back on the homebound trail and the noises of civilization. She wanted the freedom to explore the valleys of her own existence. That's what she wanted to do, to find the deepest silence, even if she got lost, walking alone now.

Her fingers were wet, as much from the desire to please herself as to seduce him from a distance. His dildo stood beside her on the desk like a sentinel. She took it in her hand

and felt its weight and its girth, and then decided she did not need it. What she really wanted was the real thing. And maybe it was right there, across the way, hidden behind a windowpane.

She opened her eyes. She was still blindfolded by the scarf. She thought about it for a moment, and then she slipped off the scarf. She could see that the window she had focused on was now open, but no one was there behind it. There was no man looking intently at her. No Alexander gazing amorously towards her. Maybe the whole thing had played itself out in her mind, she thought. Maybe it was all nothing but a dream, a figment of her imagination. Maybe she had made up the illusion of the mysterious lover. Maybe it was the dildo all along. Maybe nothing else.

And then she saw a shadow float past. There was someone after all. She just could not figure who it was. Man or woman. Could be the maid, as far as she knew. *Dommage*, she thought in French. A shame, but also close to "damage," which is what she felt like. Somewhat damaged. Somewhat alone. And then there was a knock on the door, followed by the door opening right after the knock. She was about to jump to attention when she heard the voice say, "Stay right where you are. Just the way you are." It was the sweet, unmistakable voice of Julie. "I thought I heard some moans from the pool deck," she said. "You may not have been as quiet as you thought. . . . And I brought my camera in case you wanted some memory of this," she added as she swept her hand around the room. It was dark inside, except for a tight beam of light falling on Angelica's glowing body. She looked perfectly disheveled and naughty and innocent all at once. A painting by Balthus, thought Julie as she started taking pictures without waiting for an answer.

"Please proceed," Angelica told her quietly this time, and Julie shot the blur of the fingers against the pale white triangle that love requires. Around them, the rest of the room was in vibrant darkness. The sheets on the still-unmade bed behind the girl captured lazy rays of incoming light. On the pictures, they resonated like a beacon of things to come.

Both women were in their private bubbles, floating high above the ground. They were telling the tales of their distant pasts and the stories they most often left untold. Each was the product of an earlier encounter, of past men under different roofs, of past bliss and discontent, of lights that flickered on and off.

That was the state of Angelica's mind, and she was filled with the impulse to show it all. And Julie was ready to record it. They were a perfect match in that room, and the camera found the body and followed the traces of light and lust that streamed upon it. Between the length of her thighs, the crest of her breasts, and the outline of her face, leaning backwards and wanting, the images captured the expectancy, the yearning for the other, or for nothing.

There was a feeling of incompleteness that lingered on the

screen as Julie looked at them. She looked back out to the adjacent building some forty meters away. At the open window stood a figure with hands cupped around his face. She could see that it was a man. She was not sure though if he was looking at them with naked eyes or through a small set of binoculars. She realized that she liked it—that, whoever he was, he completed the loop by his voyeuristic presence.

She walked around the desk and whispered in Angelica's ear, "He's watching. From across the other building. From the open window."

Angelica raised her head and squinted into the light, hoping to see him beyond the window frame. She let out another small moan. She would be so ready for him if he was there. She wanted to gesture for him to come. Instead, she sent a small wave of her free hand. She whispered back to Julie, "Fuck me with this," as she handed her the dildo. "Hard."

THEY WERE READY TO LEAVE as soon as the act was done. Angelica was definitely not ready to bump into Helena yet. They got into the car, and Jim drove with Julie by his side while Angelica spread herself in the backseat. "Where to?" asked Jim.

"Hotel du Cap first," said Angelica. "I've made reservations for lunch." They drove in silence at first; then Julie played Lou Doillon. She thought she had seen the singer at the Colombe d'Or.

Jim drove fast but smoothly, changing gears expertly before cruising through the turns, and the car seemed to glide all the way down towards the ocean. They were moving south through luscious green country, and the houses grew denser as they got closer to the beaches. Jim rolled the windows down, letting the warm fragrant air pour into the car. Julie, her hand on her neck, suddenly missed her long hair and the way it floated in the wind. That was long ago. Or yesterday. But then again, she was happy here. Lou Doillon was singing about seeing her love in every passing cab. The words floated around Julie. She could relate to them, but she would not willingly let Henry's shadow follow her everywhere. He didn't need to. She was going to live it and do it for her own sake.

They got to the restaurant of the Palace Hotel, by the pool, and Jim at once took his shirt and pants off as he walked towards the edge of the outdoor terrace. He took three more steps and, before anyone could stop him, he jumped off a high rock into the beautifully clear and salty sea. The cool Mediterranean water blissfully surrounded him as he blew bubbles all the way back up. He smiled broadly to the girls who were looking down at him, then waved and went off for his swim.

The ladies watched him swim away and turned toward the pool. They fooled the young security guy at the gate and walked right to the private pool area as if they owned the place. They were beautiful, and in a place like that it's all that matters. This was the home of the sybarites, the rich ones, who could indulge in the excessive prices that kept the riffraff out. And here they loved beautiful women, seeking them from behind the dark lenses of sunglasses. These men were all tanned and relaxed, searching for another layer of exclusive pleasure. Julie and Angelica fit that bill, especially when they both disrobed to their small bikinis and elegantly entered the pale blue water of the pool.

From the edge of it, they could see the iconic rope ladder, straight rope, and trapeze that hung side by the side over the dark blue sea. They were taking in the luxury yachts floating nearby and the giant black tenders that brought new visitors to the Eden-Roc when they saw Jim swimming towards them. He did not break stride and came right under the trapeze and the other gymnastic elements. He had seen pictures of them in advertising campaigns in the past and he had always wanted to climb up there. A quick snap of his legs propelled him out of the water high enough to grab the single knotted rope. Julie watched him as he climbed fast and steadily. On-lookers from the restaurant and the pool deck watched as well. Few people ever ventured on the gymnastic elements, for they were high above the water and all eyes would be on whoever used them.

He reached the top and moved to the wooden trapeze, his body dripping saltwater into the waves beneath him. He looked up and saw the girls, but his eyes were only on Julie as he let his torso fall behind him. She gasped for a second until she realized that he was safely hanging from his bent knees.

His shape was marvelous against the dark background. She wished she had a camera right then. Often, she caught herself wishing for that, to be able to capture those instances that lasted for mere seconds and then vanished. Jim took one more look at them and let his knees release him like a straight arrow into the moving water.

Julie had to restrain herself to not clap out loud. She liked Jim, not only because he did such unusual things, pushing the envelope each time, but also because he did it with style. The climbing of the trapeze did not matter really; the style did though, and she loved him even more for that, right there. And then she turned around to see if Angelica had seen it all as well.

She, Angelica of the fateful destiny, had taken her top off and, her back to the ocean, was facing the pool deck. Julie recognized that smile—the same smile she gave them whenever they took pictures of her—and for the second time that day wished she had a camera right there and then. That too would have been a perfect shot. The pale blue pool with the vibrant brunette displaying for all to see the seductiveness of her slender body, facing the wealthy elite that had it all. . .all, but not her, not Angelica. At least not yet.

Julie's face lit up when she saw Jim appear at the side of the pool with his camera in hand, taking pictures. Slowly, very quietly, she separated herself from Angelica and swam underwater to the steps that led her, three steps later, beside Jim.

"How did you get here so fast?" she asked.

"Last thing I saw before I took the dive was the top being removed! And I knew it was going to be good, so I swam as fast as I could to our bags. Now, take over," he said handing her the camera.

"No, you do it," she answered.

"Go ahead," he said. "My hands are still wet. Can't grab it so well."

He knew, and she knew, that she would capture the essence of that unusual moment with far more ease than Jim ever could. And she did.

Angelica walked out, dripping water and sensuality, and the three of them sat down for a light lunch. The bill was picked up by a stranger, and they did not wait to find out who it was. Instead, they hurried back to the car and started driving toward home, laughing aloud like teenagers.

On the way back they stopped by the Musée Picasso of Antibes. The paintings were glorious, but what really struck them was an oversized canvas by Nicolas de Stael, the strokes of color becoming for each a pathway into their own individual souls. He had painted in Antibes. Had taken his life there as well—and left behind his message of love spread all over his paintings.

After the museum, they had a cup of coffee at a café close by, drinking the espressos from small colorful cups. "From Vallauris," said the waiter when Jim asked him where they came from. Later, when they got back to the car, he settled into the driver's seat and pulled cups from his deep pockets. He handed each of them her own "borrowed" cup, a red one for Angelica and a deep orange one for Julie. Little bits of color, as if scooped away from de Stael's canvas.

Angelica was in the back seat again, and they had the Rolling Stones playing the entire trip back. At times, the three of them sang as loud as they could. Angelica was grateful for the distraction. For some reason, she felt nervous about going back there. To the hotel. To Helena and then, maybe, to Alexander, and who knew what else? But then again, how can you worry when you're singing "I Can Get No Satisfaction" as loud as possible from a fast-moving car?

They traveled with windows wide open through the lush countryside. An hour later, they were back in their respective rooms. It was good to be back, to take a shower, to find the depth of the day mixed into the echo of one's soul, and maybe even to get a glimpse of the mother soul—the initial one. Each soul has to climb back through its life towards the initial one, and, along the way, it may get help from other souls that belong to the same trunk. Sometimes these are living beings one meets along our life, and at other times they are souls that have departed but are fueled by our own actions.

The three of them were of the same trunk—Jim with his antics, his jumps, his smooth driving, his manly behavior; Angelica with her thirst, and display, and overall sense of the drama without being tragic; and Julie, with her photos, and the way she ran in the mornings, and the fellatio she was giving the clean and freshly shaved Jim while he rested on their bed with a camera in hand framing the incredible sight in the waning hours of the day.

"I never want this day to end," said Angelica when they all met for dinner.

"It may not end anytime soon," said Julie, pointing her gaze to a nearby table where Helena and Alexander were sitting, facing each other. Angelica could see that they were deep in conversation, with Helena seemingly arguing while Alexander listened on. Helena looked beautiful. She always did. That was part of her problem. Her proportions and entire being were explicitly perfect. Her face symmetrical, her eyebrows evenly arched, her shoulders sloping gracefully to heavy, luscious breasts. She was dressed in a pleated pale blue dress with narrow straps that spanned her chest. Her hair was drawn up in a small bun. Very Greek-goddess looking, thought Angelica, which was a riot since she was the one who was the closest to such divine ancestry. She looked at Alexander again. A while back, she had turned down his advances, even after he had fallen for her ever so deeply. She had turned down his proposal to settle down with him and to perhaps raise a family. She had turned it down, not out of spite, but from fear of losing her freedom.

He had been so forlorn and alone after she rejected him that she felt she had to introduce him to Helena. They had seemed to hit it off at once. What Angelica had failed to realize was that he stayed with Helena for her sake, for her to see how good a man he was and how happy he could make someone. But Angelica all but ignored him, and because he was so in love with her, he had been forced to find another way to reach her. Hence the "mysterious lover" with pearls, gimmicks, airline tickets, and blindfolds.

Often, in those early days back home, Alexander sat with legs crossed on the pale green carpet he kept in his room and let his mind go quiet in meditation in an attempt to find her. She was elusive, but he rarely failed to find her in the visions of his inner being. She was there, waiting to be captured. And then she was gone. And maybe she had never been there. He always wondered if these intense meditations had any effect on her being, on her life, on her thoughts. Did Angelica feel even an inkling of him? He surely hoped so. He wanted her to, but he could not reveal himself to her again. Repeated rejection was too painful.

So he became anonymous, appealing to her sense of adventure. He did it to a fault, at the risk of losing the love he had for her, of losing the respect he still had for her. How could he love someone who had turned him down but accepted the advances of a total stranger? But then again, somewhere in the deep recesses of his mind, that aspect of her satisfied him. What would Freud say? He could not care less. Pleasure analyzed is no longer any pleasure. Maybe later in life, he would think about it. For now, he was just happy to catch a glimpse of her while he faced Helena at the table.

Helena eventually noticed his inattentiveness, and she turned around to see what was distracting him. She saw the three of them, Jim, Julie, and Angelica, sitting and laughing at a round table, and without another word to Alexander, she got up and took a seat next to them.

"Wow! So good to have you here," said Angelica. They proceeded to explain what they had done today and "wasn't the South of France just the best!" and so forth. Angelica looked up; Alexander had left the room. Helena was now asking Julie if she could help her put together a model's portfolio. She did not notice Angelica slip away silently.

ANGELICA WAS THINKING ABOUT ALEXANDER, on the way back to her room above the pool, as she never had before. Even days earlier, when she believed it might be him who found her blindfolded in her room up in the abandoned convent, she had not thought of him very seriously—it was as if she had needed to see his face again to capture the full emotion of his presence. And she had been shocked. She had never remembered him so handsome, so present. She had been stunned by how intelligent his face appeared and how gracefully his hands moved. The darkness of their lovemaking had suddenly shed new light on all his features, and she had responded to it. She could feel it, in the flush of her face, in the heat deep within her. She wanted more now and as she mounted the stairs, wished so hard that there was someone by the window across her room, and that that someone would be Alexander. The pool was empty as she looked out, empty and quiet in its ethereal opalescent emerald glow.

She was standing by her open balcony doors, her loose white dress shining bright in the surrounding darkness of the stonewall and the dark leaves of the climbing ivy. Her body was quivering with anticipation. No blindfolds, no walls, just empty space between her and the other window. It was closed, though. She could not believe it. "Have I been wrong all along?" she mumbled once again to herself. She shut her eyes against his absence and pressed her eyelids hard, feeling the burn. When her gaze returned, she saw the pane of the window open up. It was like a wave of silver light from afar, with the vintage glass pivoting into the moonlight and revealing the figure of Alexander, standing silently.

He was wearing the dark blue shirt he had worn at dinner, but it was unbuttoned, revealing his chest and more. She felt she had to do something as well. She untied the straps of her dress and let it slide down to her hips, exposing her white lace balconette. He just looked at her. She could feel his gaze rather than see it. She could feel it as it pierced through the air to reach her and begged her for more. And she did not fail. She moved her hips from side to side and let the dress slip further down. Then she seized her cellphone and, with the dim light of the screen, painted her body with light, revealing the lace on top and her nakedness down below. She let the light sweep up and down and side to side, revealing in slow motion all the emotions of her wanting body. She wanted him to see it, see the full intensity of her segmented nakedness. She projected herself like a stripper bathed in light and, in her mind, she saw both of them reach each other over the pool and kiss a long kiss that slowly spiraled down into the water. She looked at him, and at the pool, and him again.

She wanted so much for them to be in the evening water, to float towards each other and find limbs in the darkness. More than anything, she wanted him to lie down on the still warm stones by the side of the swimming pool, and to take him in her mouth and make him grow as big as she knew he could become. She closed her eyes again and saw herself get satisfied with all he had to offer—hard, soft, full or cavernous. She wanted to bring him close to the brink and then settle on him. Her mind, so romantically inclined moments ago, was now feeding her impure thoughts, one more daring than the other. She still wished for a meeting of the souls but now through the gates of the flesh. Something that would raise the desire of all things and all beings. She wanted to volunteer—no, to sacrifice—her body in the doing. To lead the path of absolute devotion to the other. To melt into his arms, his being. To be his.

And then, she opened her eyes again, climbed out of her vision of future decadence, and watched, in the candlelight he must have lit, Helena leaning forward onto him and performing all the magic she had planned to do.

TWELVE

J ULIE WAS BACK IN HER ROOM with Jim. He was washing up, and she had quickly removed her panties from under the linen skirt she was wearing. She was smiling at herself, thinking of what a teenager she was becoming on this trip, when she heard her phone ping. This can't wait, she thought as she saw the door of the bathroom open and she lay back on the bed, the slit of her dress opened just so. Jim got closer in the dim light, shirtless and the top button of his blue jeans undone, just like in the movies.

Her phone pinged again. He got closer. It pinged once more. She reached for it and quickly read the messages as he sat at her feet and started caressing them. She scrolled down on the screen, and he lifted her foot up to his mouth, widening the gap of her dress and exposing more and more of her naked leg. He kind of liked it, to be there, satisfying her as she was all business on her phone. It felt strangely acceptable, even inviting. The fullness of her big toe upon his lips, his mouth about ready to engulf it when she finally had a little laugh and said, "You have got to see this," and handed him the phone.

The first message was from the townhouse couple they had photographed back in New York City with the wife in various iterations of a fantasy world. It read, *We saw you are in South of France on your Instagram feed. Please join us in Cadaqués. It's a charming fisherman village ninety minutes north of Barcelona by car. We have a big house overlooking the Mediterranean and extra rooms. Bring a friend if you want. Definitely bring Jim. Please say yes. We will take care of the logistics. Meet us tomorrow?*

The next one was from Angelica. It read, *Wow. Wait till I tell you what I just witnessed. . .I need to leave this place, most likely early tomorrow morning. Not sure where yet, but I'm sure that it will sort itself out. It always does. You can come along or stay. The room is yours for a few more days if you want.*

THIRTEEN

HOW DO YOU DEAL WITH YOUR ANIMAL SELF? Do you do everything you can to subjugate it and live in a meditative cloister by choice, or can it become the vehicle that leads you to higher grounds? More importantly, which of these options is the best for you?

The sunlight sliced through the window of the car every time it made a left turn on the road up the small mountain. Jim was driving again, curving the small SUV along the edge of the narrow road. Julie could feel the heat of the sun on her naked arm. It came and went as the turns took them from shadow to warm brightness. The rocks were beautiful, with shapes as varied as the clouds in the sky.

They reached the mountaintop, and suddenly the sun was everywhere, almost blinding them, almost obscuring the beautiful expanse of dark blue water that lay ahead of them.

"Oh, my goodness," came the voice from the backseat. "It's fantastic!"

"And there's Cadaqués in the distance," Angelica added as the white houses of the harbor came into view. The car was flowing down the road now, with Jim using the full span of the narrow strip of asphalt. In, close to the edge, he went around the bend and then out onto the other side of the road as he came out of the turns. In, out. Gears shifting. Music pumping. The women so excited by the sight of the sea and the lack of sleep. All of it happened really fast. They had left the hotel, La Colombe d'Or, at dawn before any guests were up and the breakfast tables by the courtyard even set up, before Alexander could see them leave. The rented SUV was waiting for them in Barcelona as they got off the plane from Nice, and barely hours after leaving the hotel, they were moments away from settling down into a new house—and a new set of circumstances and consequences. The car windows were all wide open, and loud reggae music was playing. They were like lightning rolling down to the sea, like bolts of love and desire ready to fall upon the quiet house of the couple who had invited them.

"Tell me again, where are we going? Who are these people?" asked Angelica, swaying her body to Bob Marley's "Is This Love?".

"We took pictures of them, actually mainly the wife, a

while back. Let's just say that they're not your ordinary couple, and not only because they are super wealthy," Julie
pointed out as she turned around and looked at Angelica with
a glint in her eye.

"Well, that made it as clear as mud!" Angelica laughed.

Before long, they reached the outskirts of the small town.

"You must be kidding me!" Jim muttered under his breath
as the GPS had him go through streets so narrow that the side
mirrors had to be retracted. It almost felt as if they had to slip
through some kind of physical gauntlet before reaching the ultimate escape.

Eventually they made it to the house, and it was lovely. It
rested on the left side of the bay, away from the town houses
and separated by tall pines from their neighbors. A low stone
wall outlined a garden and followed the edge of the coast.
They drove through the gate, and Angelica at once said, "I love
it! I love the smell!"

She is so right, thought Julie. There was magic in the scent
of the sea and the whispering pines. It was a scent that elevated
the soul— "that makes life worth living," Julie sighed as she
inhaled deeper. And living well is what they all wanted —to
live to the full extent of each hour, to smell the gardens by the
sea and reach a plenitude, not merely to perceive the scent of
crystallized nature, but to let it penetrate deep. And just then,
the fragrant air engulfed them in an invisible link with each
breath, linked them to each other as well as to the man who

was appearing from the house to greet them.

He was obviously excited. His wife, Shari, followed seconds later. It felt deliberate, as if she had wanted to separate herself a little from her husband.

She loved him, there was no doubt about that. She loved him mightily and loved every moment they spent together, but she also loved those few seconds she had placed between the two of them as they greeted their new guests.

Julie and Jim looked at each other for the shortest moment and smiled. It was a smile of complicity and knowledge. They had both tasted the wife at different intervals not long before and here she was, lingering between them in a dizzying aura that required no explanation.

Shari looked up at a beautifully bright butterfly displaying its open wings as it floated by. "Oh!" she exclaimed, "so special! Never seen a butterfly here yet."

Julie smiled, the smallest of genuine smiles, and looked at the air around her. Yes, Henry. I see you. I know you're here. With that, she kissed and hugged Shari. She was really happy to see her again. In many ways, she truly was like an old friend. After all, over the past few weeks, she had photographed her in the most intimate of ways and then, in turn, been photographed with her. The power of capturing and being captured linked them in a feral way. Shari felt it as well. Words were not needed, the two of them like mountain climbers who, having reached a summit together, have a bond

between them that no one else can share. Not even Shari's husband, Daniel. Even if he was the one who eventually saw it
all unravel. Even though he was the one who had started the
whole affair—letting it blossom out of an inner desire that he
could not explain. Daniel had often thought about that, about
the possible reasons that made him ask for the escapades of
his wife, facilitate them—and ultimately enjoy it. He had dis-
cussed it with her, his Shari of the strong eyes and the endless
smile. Maybe it was to show her off, to reveal her to the ultimate degree to strangers, almost as an act of defiance and
abandon. Some might see it as weakness, as him having to give
his wife away so she could finally get sexually rewarded. But
that was far from the truth. He had an almost ideal sensual
life with Shari, in bed and outside it. They were always hungry, always ready for each other. So it was not weakness.
"Maybe," he had told her, "it was the idea of absolute possession." Of being able to tell her what to do, whom to open to.
He knew that the ultimate reason would most likely remain
unknown but it certainly was done for the sake of the story:
for the value of the narrative, for the retelling of it between
soft sheets in a dark room as she admitted in quiet whispers
all the excesses she had offered and all the unspeakable acts
she had performed for him. It was pure delight to him. There
was no jealousy involved, only respect for her wondrous behavior.

Therefore it was an interesting handshake to have with

Jim—the visual of the young man's fingers deep in his wife still resonating in Daniel's being. He kept the hand wrapped in his for just a fraction longer than necessary, almost as a sign of acknowledgement. Jim noticed that and squeezed a little harder, as an accomplice would, with a hint of a smile on his lips. With the reunion over, they introduced Angelica, charming as expected, to the couple.

Then Shari led them all to a hidden veranda behind the house, and they sat down for lunch at a long table nestled under a gazebo covered with purple bougainvillea. The white wine was served in large round glasses filled with ice, and you had to drink it fast before it got watered down. The food was delicious, and they ate and laughed while the local chef kept bringing small dishes for them to taste. There were tapas of various textures and flavors, from food fresh out of the sea to smoked meats and other local delicacies. Jim ate all of the small portions, but he was still starving. He finished the tortilla, the bread, and the untouched olives, but soon enough he realized that he was not going to feel satiated by this meal. He made peace with it, thinking of the long open-water swim he had already planned.

"After this, let's go on the boat for a quick ride. If you want to, of course," suggested Daniel. "Maybe after a little siesta?"

They were all far too excited to think about sleep. "Yes, a boat ride sounds just great," answered Julie. "Let's skip the siesta and keep it for tonight!"

The boat they had rented with the house was a gift Dalí had given Gala, his wife and muse, in the days when they lived in Cadaqués. It was a long wooden craft painted yellow on the outside and pale blue on the inside. The name *Gala* was painted in dark letters on each side, with a big G and a big L, and the two a's in small letters, as if a child had painted it. Most likely it had been Dalí himself, as if hiding a message— GL for "Good Life." It reminded Julie of Living Well is the Best Revenge, the book that she and Angelica were now reading simultaneously—sometimes together, if one caught up with the other.

Once in the boat, they picked up Jim, who had gone swimming ahead way before the others left. They motored around the tip of the harbor and followed the coast for a while, the pale-red rocks catching the slowly waning sun in their crevices. They went into another bay, and Shari pointed out Dalí's house, the one with the giant egg sculptures. She showed them how he had bought a number of fishermen's huts in the Thirties and linked them to build his own seaside villa, complete with multiple terraces, and row upon row of olive trees. You could still feel his presence there, surrounded by the beauty of the bay and the omnipresent vanity of his wife.

The boat made a graceful arc around the small harbor and went back out towards the sea. They traveled up north a little further, long enough for Jim to scout future swims and for clouds to gather along the horizon. "Uh-oh! We better go back now. That is rain you see over there," said Daniel as he pointed to what looked like pencil drawings in various shades of grey stretched between the sky and the sea. The wind picked up. The waves curled in, and small white crests appeared on top of them.

The three women were sitting up front, chatting away. Jim and Daniel were at the back of the boat with Daniel holding the tiller. The two men were quiet in the knowledge of what had happened between Jim and Shari, and in the understanding that Daniel had not only approved but instigated it. In front of them, the view of the boat, carrying along the waves the three women dressed in various iterations of white, had a movie quality to it. Angelica was in a long strapless dress, Julie in shorts and a low-cut T-shirt, and Shari wore a tennis outfit. It was like a Botticelli painting, thought Daniel, as the light streamed from the sea below and all around dark clouds rapidly gained on them. "Charm, beauty, and elegance," he said to Jim, pointing to the women with a nod.

"Yes," said Jim, who was also thinking about that. "The Three Graces," he added.

"Soon to be the Three Wet Graces!" laughed Daniel as he saw the shadow of raindrops following them ever so closely. The rain came down soft and wet, warm in the summer moment, and the women became girls again. They tilted their heads back and the drops flowed on their smiling faces and open mouths like manna from the sky. The sea around them was suddenly quieted by the raindrops drawing circles on its steaming surface.

Soon the girls were drenched. There was no way to avoid it. The wet fabric stuck to their bodies in smooth white out-lines, as if a painter's brush had traced their exposed flesh. Jim took his camera out and caught them, more naked than nude, as the sun reemerged on the other side of the sky. He caught Shari's large, sensuous nipples stuck to her shirt, and Angelica's hips enhanced by her wet dress, as well as the tightness of Julie's core as the drenched t-shirt clung to her. Hair wet and lips red with laughter, they looked superb, both in the boat and on the screen. "Faster!" they said to Daniel, as if they wanted to re-enter the warmth of the divine rain shower that preceded them as if announcing the tabernacle. Suddenly, the returning sunlight caught up with the bright yellow shell of the *Gala*, and it became, for a suspended moment, a miniature sun float-ing along a coast of angels.

Daniel was looking pensively at the ever-changing sea, thinking about the unexpected rainfall he saw as a shower of purification, an absolution of sorts, for all things done and all that was yet to come. The passing rainfall had been like sex as well, he thought, seeing how it had hovered above all of them and eventually undressed the women. Even more, he re-flected, the downpour seemed to have cleared a layer of their souls, and their own mutual laughter in the boat had revealed yet another. He knew, from all his years of studying, that layer by layer they were meant to eventually shed them all—the layers of ego, and the ones of false prophecies, and the ones of unfounded expectations. He sighed, almost in prayer, wishing to get closer to the infinite oneness he'd been searching for, for so long.

They were still laughing after the boat was moored and as they ran back home, shoes in hand and eyes gleaming.

FOURTEEN

A LITTLE LATER, WHILE WAITING for the others to show up, Jim picked up a book left partially open on a low table in the living room. Without really knowing why, he took a deep breath of it, inhaling the scent of the old pages. It smelled incredibly good, a feminine scent he instantly recognized. "The perfume of my first girlfriend," he said to no one in particular. The book was by a certain Moshe Chaim Luzzatto. The inside cover announced him as a brilliant young 18th- century kabbalist. Jim had never heard about Kabbalah. He read on, leaning against the window overlooking the harbor. They were going out for dinner. It was late already, but it appeared that it was not late enough for Spain. They had to wait a little longer before they could set off.

The book was about the mystic's attempt to separate himself

from earthly desire and pleasure in order to access another realm. That was a concept Jim was familiar with: Christian monks, Buddhist monks, nuns, Dervishes, all seemed to adhere to those principles of self-denial. Yet he, personally, could not. He understood the need to seek transcendence and avoid animalistic behavior, but still he wondered, Why would the Almighty provide humans with the perfection of the human body if it was not to use it to its fullest effectiveness? In his core he did intuitively understand, as the writer described it, the separation between base pleasure and enlightened pleasure, and how it relied on the awareness of the moment and the zeal with which the moment was appreciated. But then again, death will eventually come, and with it the ultimate separation of body and soul, he reflected as he looked out at the harbor. For the moment, at least, he wished for nothing else but to continue to ride the waves of physical pleasure, like a surfer reaching out for the beach, steady on his board and master of the wave—his body both wave and board.

He knew the book he held in his hands was filled with truths. How else could it emanate such a scent? But he also was glad that he was too raw a man for its ultimate reasoning.

Julie approached him silently and laid a hand on his shoulder. "What are you reading, cowboy?" she asked teasingly.

"A book I found here on the table," he said. "Take a whiff of it."

She did. "Oh, my!" she said, blushing slightly. "It smells like Henry!"

Jim said nothing. There was nothing to be said.

"Ah! I see you found my book," Daniel called out. "I must have left it here earlier."

"Where did you get it?" asked Jim.

"Well, I didn't. Funny thing is, it got me!" Daniel reached for the book and ran his fingers along the spine. " I once bought a fantastic cabinet by Ruhlmann, and when I finally had it installed at home in the city, I found this book tucked deep against one of the inside shelves. Must have been forgotten there by the previous owner, I guess," he told them.

He did not tell them that he never traveled without the book, as much for its words of wisdom as for its mere presence— its weight, the quality of the thick paper, and of course its scent that seemed to shift whenever his mood did.

"Come, let's eat," he said. "It's finally late enough to go out!"

Angelica and Shari were waiting out in the garden, talking as if they were friends from long before. . .and maybe they were.

FIFTEEN

J ULIE WAS GOING TO WALK OVER to the harbor-side restaurant with the boys while the other two women were
driven there. "High heels oblige!" said Shari as she
waved. "We'll get the table ready," she added as the open car
pulled ahead.

At the restaurant, both women ordered Aperol spritzes, the
drinks a perfect shade of gold in the late sunset. They were
seated face to face at a table by the edge of the stone pier.
Close to them, the evening sea had turned a dark orange. It
was almost red at some places, almost purple at the crests of
the small waves. Shari knew that way up under the sky, high
above the clouds; the sun was still bright and yellow and
curved all the light. But who cared about that reality? She was
below the cover of the clouds, in a world of moving crimsons,

and closer to Angelica than she ever thought possible. They exchanged glances among their words and even a furtive but slow touch of fingers along the stem of a glass. She was at peace, sitting with beautiful Angelica as the sky silently shifted into night.

"Well!" exclaimed Daniel, seeing the empty glasses on the table. "It seems like the party has begun!" He looked at his wife. She was resplendent, dressed in shades of light, her warm dark eyes flickering for him when he smiled at her. And she smiled back, her lips glowing with a myriad of unspoken words as well as unknown acts of future decadence. They were full, warm, red, and desirable. Waiting to be offered. Waiting to be taken. He was transported by her beauty and how she shone for him like an icon of bliss. He loved her too much, he thought. Even more than their own children, he admitted, smiling at the blasphemy.

They had a lively dinner, talking all together about the day and the circumstances that had brought them all there. Angelica made them laugh through the night with impersonations of past tales and accents. Julie remained quiet and serene, registering everything and allowing the evening to gain substance by the mere weight of her attention and her photographic gaze.

They were just finishing the white fish, cooked in a light citrus broth and paired with a crisp white wine that tasted of local rocks, when the *Gala* moored right beside them. Shari, who was closest to the edge of the pier, extended her hand to the captain. She greeted him by name and, in fluent Spanish, thanked him for arriving on time. "Come aboard," she told the rest of the table. Daniel was stunned. He was the one who usually arranged such things. A stroke of genius, he thought. Then his meticulous side kicked in and he told his wife, "Darling, we're not quite done. We still need desserts and such."

"Desserts are to be served elsewhere," she said with a mysterious smile and a hint of pleasure, delighted that she had managed to surprise even him.

One by one they made their way onboard. "The check has been taken care of as well," she told Daniel when it was his turn to board. Finally, she joined them, her heels sonorous on the quiet wooden hull. The captain started the engine again and after one last push from the rocky pier they were off towards deeper darkness.

She must have planned dessert at home, thought Daniel. But the *Gala* was not headed toward the house, rather it was going in the opposite direction, aiming for the distant lighthouse. They steadily moved away from shore, their immediate surroundings becoming darker and darker with each passing moment and the presence of the town slowly melting away behind them. The sudden outline of a sloop came almost as a surprise.

Looking at it, Daniel thought about his favorite artist, Barnett Newman. Maybe it was the tall mast of the beautiful craft, stretching like a zip along the sky just as the artist painted them on his canvases. Or maybe it was the incredible blend of dark blues and black—the very essence of those pigments, or the absence of them, sinking deep into him as if filling a void.

The sea was calm, and the ship barely swayed. A sailor on the sail boat greeted them and turned on the deck lights, revealing beautiful teak floorboards tightly laid against each other, like the lines of a story yet to be told. They took their shoes off, feeling with their bare feet the smoothness of the honed and scrubbed wood. Coils of thick white rope rested along the side of the deck like creatures awaiting their turn. Holding a lantern, the sailor led them to a lounging area toward the middle of the boat, behind the shiny steering wheels. He lit candles, showed Daniel where the bar was, and then left on the *Gala* with his mate.

Angelica felt under her feet the softness of the fabric that covered the floor of the sunken lounge area. She also felt, to her surprise, that she missed Alexander from Paris right now. It was the first time she had thought about him in a long while, and it struck her hard. She looked up at the tall mast in the moonless night pointed resolutely to the heavens. Two planets were out, side by side, bright Jupiter and distant Saturn. She knew it because Jim had checked earlier with an app on his phone. She wondered if that was a good omen. A gust of wind brought from shore a burst of heat laced with the scent of pine. The slowly moving mast waved to the planets. Like a dance, she told herself. It was all good, she decided as she started moving her hips.

Jim had put on music, a blend of guitar and rhythms that favored that part of the world. She recognized the opening notes—the Gutierrez Brothers, maybe? It was very danceable. Jim had picked well. She closed her eyes and got submerged in it, letting her waist trace the melody in the fragrant air. She wore elegant dark red shorts that showed off her long legs. In her hand she had the drink Daniel had made for all of them. It was a smoky type of Margarita, sweet but not sugary and easy to swallow. She could feel the mescal sinking deeper in her, like magic fueling her moves, and her hips swayed lazily in the flickering candlelight, foreshadowing their potential.

Gradually, the rhythm of the dance got faster, blending with the harmony of the waves licking the side of the boat's keel.

Shari got up and joined her. Their legs grazed through the slit of Shari's dress and then their hands touched again, and their arms interlocked. As the song spread itself through their isolated enclave, their hips joined, facing each other as they moved in unison, oblivious to the skies and the three others. The darkness of their locked eyes was like brilliant wings in the night and, bathed in dim light, they gradually linked against each other, delicate flesh upon delicate frame. Lost in the music and rocked by the motion of the sea they carved, in the warm air, the aura of an early trance, the onset of a bacchanal.

Julie wore a long silk dress, dark green with thin golden threads that molded her body like a second skin. She had never worn it before—the hidden nakedness of it seemed almost too much for her. But Jim had insisted, and so she had it on, for him. As the evening went by, she eventually realized that she quite enjoyed wearing it. It made her feel different. Even think differently—as if the garment had the intrinsic power to modulate her mood. She found herself moving differently in it. More seductively. Her shoulders arched back, her neck proud, and the shadow of her nipples became visible under the smooth fabric. She liked it quite a bit. It seemed to transform her, as if she was entering a new world.

She moved to the bar. Slowly, she refilled her glass, the cocktail pouring thick over the large ice cubes. Taking a sip of the drink, she watched the men, their eyes fixed intently on Angelica and Shari's luscious dance. She let the glass rest on her lips for a while, the same way she would let Henry's hand rest on her body at night as he slept beside her. Her body had belonged to him for so long it had become partially his as well. And she liked it that way, had given it over to him, bit by bit, like the time he had blindfolded her and, to her surprise, run the sharp tip of a blade along her naked skin. That night, his hand had been light and gentle, leaving only the trace of a thin line. It was all so far away now, that scar barely visible. Looking at the tabletop, she noticed the small, sharp knife with which Daniel had sliced the limes for the drinks and, without thinking, she picked it up and, remembering Henry, gently ran it over her dress. The blade moved, and when the sharp edge caught the thin silk, she found herself letting it slice the fabric from breast to hips. All the while, she kept her gaze fixed on the two men seated in the corner of the plush area. They too stared at her now, mesmerized, looking on as the blade ran easily along the dark silk, revealing her sun-kissed skin. The blade then hit the two shoulder straps, freeing up the dress. Her body taut, she let it slide down. It hugged her hips for an instant and then gathered in a green and gold heap by her bare feet. The same blade sliced through the sides of her black thong as she took the few steps that separated her from the seated men. At all times, her eyes never stopped capturing the photographic vision of it—from the shimmer of the candlelight that exposed the skin of the dancing bodies, to the glow of Jim's eyes. That same glow she found in Daniel's eyes as she got closer to him.

DANIEL TOOK IT ALL IN. First his wife, smiling at him as she kept moving in rhythm, then the hips of Julie, naked, bare, and swinging in synch with the giant mast, obscuring it completely when she stood right in front of him in all her nakedness. That is when Jim pushed her just a little further with his hand, pushing her to straddle Daniel's smiling face. Her hips reached Daniel's mouth and his tongue went searching, finding without fail the sea and the stars within her.

Jim, shirtless, was standing beside her. She could feel his chest against her nudity, his mouth moving from her shoulder to the side of her breast, then slowly tracing her hips and traveling south. Sweet shivers hurried up her spine when she felt his teeth as he gently bit the roundness of her ass. She spread her legs some more, angling towards him. He did not disobey either. His tongue found her savory side and from both ends she fed them her nectar. With a hand on each head, Julie looked up in the skies and saw the glitter that invisibly links all planets and distant lights. Her shoulders arched further back, and with her hair seemingly long again, she thought she could feel the ends of her blonde curls on her skin. And then, when time had seemed to suspend itself, it was Shari's turn to find her and mix tongues with her, as the numbers of fate kept unscrolling all around them.

Shirts and pants were discarded, and flesh found flesh upon skin, the softness of women stumbling upon the edges of the men. Angelica was still alone, dancing in the middle of the lounge. Somehow her high heels were back on, and she moved gracefully, taller than her frame, her see-through shirt slicing the translucid night away. She twirled, her beauty following her in the warm air. All the while, she kept her eyes closed and for a moment she was a little girl again, hopping from stone to stone along a path back in Greece, following her mother's footsteps. Why that memory, that vision? Why just then? She could not tell. Her feet were close together, and she swayed more than she danced, all the impulses of her being caught in the splendor of her smiling face. Oblivious to her carnal surroundings, her body was moving ever so slowly, as if preparing itself. When Daniel captured her hand and pulled her down, she spread herself on the ground like water on hot cement. Hands hauled her in and brought her closer. She could smell the musk of men, and with her eyes closed, could not tell which, but she knew she wanted them.

The wind blew the sound of their music further out to the sea. It blew with it a vision of Angelica tied up with thin maritime ropes, spread-eagle along the covered deck, and Shari offering her all of her plenitude as she lowered herself upon her face, facing Jim who, slipping between Angelica's lower lips, split her as if into another half with his girth. He looked up and kissed Shari's mouth as they both received and gave from the fullness of their triangle. Not long after, unable only to watch, Daniel pushed Shari further down, flattening her body against Angelica's. He could not wait to take his own wife, and as he thrust into her from behind, over Angelica's open mouth, each thrust pushed her face towards Jim's action. Julie, meanwhile, freed up Angelica's legs from the ropes and the high-heeled shoes reached out towards the heavens as she started snapping pictures. She continued taking photos despite her desire to be in there with Jim. Intrinsically, she knew this was just too good not to be captured on film. She searched for the light as it travelled between the crevices of limbs and more legs and spread ass. She found it, the magical light, gliding along the glistening shafts of the men as they went about, as they moved into open shapes and as saliva dripped onto them. She saw the tales of decadence being retold with as much elegance and savagery as ever there could be. She could barely believe the stories being captured on her screen, but still she took the camera with her as she went within the linked bodies and revealed from up close the power of lips against sweet pussies and the fervor of cocks that stood their ground. Hot winds from the shore added even more heat to the scene and made sweat slip from the chest of the men onto the willing bodies. Julie's images were vivid, of fingers that made toes curl in delight, of fragrant fluids that dripped with purpose. The images captured all but the intoxicating scent of flagrant sex. When the camera went silent, they all remained motionless, spread upon the thin mattress in linked shapes of stars, each touching someone, each alone.

Later that same night, with eyes still filled with sleep and the remains of the mezcal, Daniel felt the naked body of his wife on his left. Instinctively, he reached with his hand between his legs and realized how hard he was. Maybe he had been dreaming. Maybe it was the motion of the sailboat. Maybe it was just a gift. Whatever the reason might have been, his renewed hardness made her even more desirable, and he positioned himself behind her. With eyes still closed and his hand lathering his cock with saliva, he found her, willing and open. He filled her like a glorious receptacle, his hips breathing the rhythm of her desire, opening his mind to the answers of her motion, her silent messages. Quietly, he moved faster, the noiseless union taking flight as her body seemingly asked for more. He grabbed her hair with the intent of pulling it back but when he opened his eyes, he was stunned to find his hand upon Angelica's head—his cock tight, deep in her pussy. He turned around to search for Shari, and there she was, leaning against her elbow and watching him with a smile on her face. He stopped moving, but Angelica, with her hand, reached out for him and applied pressure on the roundness of his ass, pinning it closer to her, beckoning for more. In the same instant he felt Shari's hands urging him on as well. And so he did, and he moaned as Shari's tongue, almost as a reward, slid down his back to reach its final destination, lapping like a wave the shores of his moving hips. She loved adding that pleasure for him. And in doing so she gave herself pleasure. And then even more so when she crawled along their linked bodies and settled her nudity against Angelica's. Breasts against breasts. Legs intertwined. Both feeling Daniel's passionate thrusts and the scent of his flesh.

By then, staying quiet no longer made sense. Etched on the surface of the still distant raising sun, Daniel could see the profile of Julie sitting and sliding on Jim, like a totem of ancient lore that needed to be repeated and recreated. The mellow hum from their hips welcomed the onset of dawn. Shari reached out with her hand, curious to feel the vigor of Jim as he stood fully erect, and along his girth her fingers found the wetness of present and recent sex. She rubbed them along Angelica's upper lip, and that fragrance, that scent, filled with all that had already happened this night, triggered a renewed dance of the flesh. Daniel, feeling the new urge, moved faster and deeper. Julie let herself slip between the linked ladies, dismounting Jim as one would a horse after a long ride. None of them were on firm ground any longer, and under the spell of their union the mast could be seen swaying, moving like a long-extended finger back and forth along the still bright morning star of Venus.

The sun could not rise fast enough to witness what was happening. All of the firmament seemed to be buzzing about the harmonious coupling, or rather quintuple union, sending rainbows of secret light into the cosmos. The invisible gift kept reverberating like an echo from the wooden deck to whoever could capture it—just as Jim did on the screen of his camera, encompassing in the image the motion of his hand along his hard cock and the spray of white sperm that landed like hot wax on the willing bodies of the three linked women.

Shari was the last one in the water. Like the conductor of her own orchestra, she watched the other bodies make their way one by one in the welcoming sea. Dawn had made its real imprint by then and from the surface of the sea you could see the sun rising pink, high above them along the ridge of an ad-

jacent hill. Daniel said a blessing. Jim recalled his mother saying, "Son, there is one sunrise and one sunset every day. It's
up to you to decide whether you will witness them or not."
And he had. It was beyond belief, he thought as he dropped
deeper in the cool sea—his head submerged in a myriad of incoming rays of light that penetrated the water—the streams of
sunlight like more flesh into flesh.

He was still amazed at how it had started with Shari, who
had arranged for the *Gala* and the sailboat. What a great idea
to use a boat—it had become the perfect neutral ground, a
floating private island, where everything goes. Her will and
Angelica's seductiveness had made it happen, the few allowing
the others to achieve whatever was meant for them.

They got back on deck, climbing up a small ladder that led
to a wooden platform. The water dripped off their skin, as if
shedding with it the last vestiges of the night gone by, and soon
the light teak wood turned darker. Their bodies wrapped in
large green towels, they made their way back to the lounge.
Already, the *Gala* was on its way back to them. They could
see the yellow hull slicing through the water, spraying white
foam on both sides, the old engine revving in a rhythm lost to
newer ones, as if bringing all of them back in time, when the
surrealists, with Breton and Éluard, were vying for Gala, and
Dalí watched on.

Bags of clothes were brought on board—bathing suits and
a choice of faded sailor's t-shirts, the blue and white stripes on

the shirts like a set of new lines to write on.

But they were hungry, and the sailor chef had arranged a buffet-style table with fruits and yogurts and freshly baked goods that were still warm from the oven. There were cheeses and breads, and eggs with yolks so yellow they competed with the fast-rising sun. Shari selected the music, a piano concerto by Satie, the notes rising lightly in the air as if nudging the sun higher. On the mast the sails were swelling out as the ship got ready to launch. Boats were moving back and forth along the bay by then and no one paid attention to the fast-approaching speedboat. "The sailboat is ours for the day," said Shari. "Well, actually one day and one night. I guess the night is gone by now," she said with a smile on her face.

"Oh, what a night!" mimicked Angelica singing the Four Seasons tune in a deep-pitched voice. The music got switched to Bob Marley. "From Satie to Marley, quite the trip."

And how excellent the night had been, thought Angelica with a gleam in her eyes. But she felt somewhat alone, like a fifth wheel. From now on, she would have to be nice to all and intimate to none. Or would they take turns at her? For she knew that there would be more sex, as sure as there would be saltwater spraying the deck and skins exposed to the waves. The crew seemed professional. They had not even glanced at any of the guests for more than a second as they disembarked from the *Gala*, and she clearly did not want to seduce any of them. She was content with what had already happened. No need for more sex. She smiled again. No, it was the company she missed. The company of a man who would hold her in his arms as the sea got rougher and would whisper soft, funny words in her ears. And tell her how well she looked. That is, if she did look good! she mused. She was tempted to tell them that she was going back home with the *Gala*. The wooden boat was already preparing to leave. Her body aching from all that had happened during the night, she could easily see herself take a shower, lie down in a soft bed, and read a book until her eyes closed. Maybe she could prepare dinner for them at the house with the chef. "Aw, it sounded delish!" she said to herself. She was about to speak out. . .but a voice from within told her not to, that by doing so, by leaving, she would destroy the dynamics of the moment and that the others would not have as much fun. The group would become serious again. Two couples, and maybe some awkward moments. But five was a charm, she realized. She would be the balancing act, the entertainment, and all would want to please her, and that would keep the group cohesive, with the power that odd numbers can muster. She relinquished thoughts of leaving and went to the bigger bathroom to find a shower. At least she would get that bit done, rinse off the salt that burned the raw spots.

From within the cubicle of the shower she could hear the speedboat get ever so close before its engines stopped altogether. There was talk going on above her on deck, but the lyrics of "No Woman, No Cry" replaced the words she could have heard. She was rinsing her hair under the warm stream when the door to the shower opened. Shari was there, smiling, with that look of someone who knows something you do not. A very desirable moment of power for some, but Shari did not linger. She looked at Angelica straight in the eyes and said, "Are you ready for this?"

"Ready for what?" was the obvious answer, and she asked it. Like a chess move—king's pawn to E4.

"We just had a new passenger come on board. How he found us, I don't know, but he is resourceful, that's for sure." Bishop moves up the diagonal, sensing weakness in the pawn line.

"OK, so just tell me already," Angelica said. King castles, with rook opening a defense.

"The guy from your hotel in St. Paul de Vence. I think his name is Alexander? Well, he's here. He just came by speed-boat and asked if he could stay." Check to the Queen.

Angelica remained silent. She was thinking fast, watching time slip away drop by drop from the ends of her wet hair. She could let him go—end of game, no need to set up the pieces again. Or she could let him aboard and then act or behave in various ways, some of which might turn ugly, others possibly unbelievably happy. It was his magical apparition at the eleventh hour in the middle of nowhere that made her sacrifice her queen to the lowly bishop.

"He can stay," she told Shari, "under one condition. You must tell him what happened here last night. Spare no detail. If he wants to leave, I will totally understand it." She ran her fingers through her hair and, with eyelids fluttering, added in a soft voice, "Now, please let me finish—the conditioner is running in my eyes."

SIXTEEN

TELL ME HOW YOU TRAVEL, and I will tell you who you are. He had traveled fast and hard to get there in time. He had said his farewells to the beautiful Helena, who still could not believe that someone would walk away from her impeccable beauty. Usually, men went to war for her, and here was this guy leaving her for that no-good of a girlfriend. Who did she think she was anyway? Some kind of princess or something? Helena was forgetting Angelica had introduced her to him to begin with.

Meanwhile, in her cabin, Angelica could feel her skin tingle with anticipation as she slowly dried her body. Oh, let him stay, she thought. Let him be strong enough to forgive her, to accept her. And murmured with a self-deprecating smile, "Although having sex through the night with four other people, two of them total strangers less than a day ago, may be a tall order!"

But he did stay. He drank the cup to the last drop, so as not to let bad luck appear at a later date. He thought he knew what he was getting into, and he was going to do it. For the better and for the even better.

She appeared on deck, her long wet black hair hanging in front of her and partially hiding her, as she exited from the shadows into the light. All eyes were focused on her. And on her utmost nakedness, fully exposed except for the smallest black bikini bottom. Her oiled skin caught the sun even under the awning.

All eyes were on her. Men's and women's alike.

Check.

Mate.

SEVENTEEN

THE SAILBOAT TOOK THEM UP along the coast, and they anchored in an isolated bay. They were the only ones there. The bay was beautiful, full of morning love. The rocks, slicing into the blue water, offered a multitude of caves for birds to fly back and forth to from their high-perched nests. All was calm and sumptuous, there to be taken. Close by, the slope of the earth along the edge of the bay irresistibly led gentle waves ashore. Alexander (now in a bathing suit, and a full member of the group) and Jim took Angelica and Julie for a tour on long paddle boards. The women sat up front and the men paddled, standing behind them. As they got closer to shore, Alexander winked at Jim and went ahead towards a hidden creek. In no time, their board had rounded the corner and they found themselves alone on a small sandy beach.

There was no talk of Helena. No talk of future plans. Just his voice that told her how much he longed for her. How he had loved her from the moment he saw her and how that love had kept growing stronger with time. And yes, he knew about last night and he could deal with it—the timbre of his voice did not falter, and she knew that he was not lying. The sun shone bright on both of them, the coolness of the drying water keeping them in just the right place. He spoke to her with words, and he spoke to her with his hand as it followed, with the softest of touches, the wet outline of her reclining shape. She let herself roll back against the warm sand and took it all in: the sun with its bright early light, and the sand and earth beneath her, and she was grateful, and also thankful for the sound of the waves lapping the shore with the rhythm of infinity. His hand searched for and found her beneath the black fabric, and she was grateful for that, too. And there was one more thing: that boat, moored close by, waiting for them, and in it a table with food and drinks, and she was thankful once more. He took her from behind to keep the sand out, and she liked it. It was raw and became almost violent, and she realized she had wanted that, wanted him to take control and reclaim her from the previous night and all the others. Her moans eventually found their way to the adjacent open creek where Jim and Julie were resting, lying on smooth round pebbles.

Jim looked up at Julie and smiled. He moved closer to her.

Moments before, in the surrounding turquoise waters, among the pebbles, he had found a long smooth and oblong stone and it fit perfectly. Like the gift. He held it tight in her with one hand and with the other lathered saliva over his own shape, spreading her ass just the way she liked it. Against the warm stone Jim felt so good that gradually, almost as in a dream, she felt a deep irresistible wave of pleasure growing in her. She grabbed his thigh and, with deep breaths haltingly repeated, "Don't stop. Don't stop." He didn't.

Julie was spent and for a moment she rested her head in the curve of his welcoming chest. In the distance, Jim saw the other couple paddling back towards the boat. He had been so focused on Julie that he had not climaxed. And he was okay with that, but his anatomy blatantly was not. It was standing there, fully erect, and Julie, looking upon it said, "Oh, no! I can't leave you like this. But, darling, I just can't take you in me anymore. I'm too sore."

She stood up and was walking now to the water to bathe and relieve herself when he said, "Wait, come back here." He was still lying down on the slanted slope of the warm pebble beach. "Come here, stand over me." And she did, hiding the sun from him. "Do it," he said to her. "Do it. Let yourself go on me."

And suddenly she understood what he wanted. She thought she had done it once for Henry. Maybe he wanted more. She closed her eyes and she tried to relax. Nothing came. For the longest time it seemed like she wouldn't be able to, and then a few drops landed on Jim's belly, and he felt the full impact of each of them, and then of the hot liquid stream that now poured out of her. Of his love, his mistress. And she sprayed upon him, making sure to avoid his face, but he leaned into it and then he came in spurts of warm white fluids that poured out of him like the caps of waves on ancient paintings—all wet and hot and messy until they both dove in the water again and laughed together with all the gods and for the only one.

Daniel had bypassed the paddle-board experience. There were only two on board at any rate, and Shari had wanted to stay back to help with lunch. Instead, he had taken a dive in the deep water around the anchored boat and adjusted his swimming goggles. They had reflecting lenses that captured the sunlight at times, making strange shadows of things, just acting like small mirrors. He remembered how, as a child, with his brother, he had burned ants with a magnifying glass. He was sorry for that. He hoped he would not be punished too harshly. He swam further and further away, against the current that he had gauged from the resting position of the ship. With a powerful stroke, he swam over deep blue water and sandy bottoms until he saw seaweed lined up around a small island barely reaching the surface. He could see submarine sea life as well as he swam along, but he did not linger. It was nothing compared to the lush underwater sea life he used to

see with his brother, back when they were kids and went swimming in that same sea. It made him sad for his own kids and
what they would most likely never see again. He did not linger
and instead pushed further and reached the submerged rock.
He stood up on it for a while, waving towards the boat, but
nobody seemed to be looking. He was OK with that. He did
not need the validation of others. He knew that he was a striking figure standing out there as if he was standing at the edge
of the water, his arms raised to the sky in an act of gratitude
and prayer, the two lenses of his goggles sending rays of un-
natural light above him. He was about to shout with joy but,
carried along the surface of the sea, he heard from the far shore
the unmistakable sounds of carnal pleasure. He smiled again.
He knew that Shari had arranged it all, but he was paying for
it. So, it made him feel good that he might bring more happiness to their little enclave, this paradise. Maybe the joy would
travel into the surrounding water and the corals would grow
back to their original splendor. He dove back in, the water
cold now on his dried skin. He had not sat down on the top
of the rock, or assumed the lotus position, or purposely altered
his breath, but he felt that he had meditated. In his world he
had done the reverse of what the gurus usually taught—instead
of spending more and more time stationary to reach a deeper
meditative state, he had taught himself to reach deeper and
deeper levels of awareness faster and faster—so fast that he felt
at times as if his whole life was becoming a constant flow of

meditative moments.

As he swam away from the sunken rock, he saw the unusual underwater configuration of a narrow tunnel about two meters from the surface and five long from what he could gauge. He could have just kept on swimming. He was too old for such games. He had kids. Other people were waiting for him on the boat. Bills had to be paid. On his first dive, he just looked at one end of the natural tunnel. On the second, he explored the other end. It was doable. Tough, but doable. Now what? Go home! his being screamed. Go back to the boat. But then again, he had burned those ants with his brother. There was a price to pay for everything. He went for it.

BACK ON THE BOAT, SHARI WAS FOCUSED on preparing the food for lunch. She loved it. The chef was young but experienced. He had worked on boats already, and he was fun to be around. She stayed with him the whole time except for quick breaks to check on the phone to make sure everything was OK with the kids. She put on the same music they had listened to the previous night. It made her laugh to be leading a somewhat normal level of activity, listening to the same rhythms upon which she had fucked and sucked and gotten fingered and abused and photographed. What a world she was living in! she thought as she went on cooking. The cucumbers were her accomplices, and she winked at them before slicing them thin and fast as the chef had just taught her, standing behind her, holding her hand over the cutting knife. She knew how to do it of course, but this was more fun—so why not? And it would be fun to tell Daniel.

Where was he? she wondered. The others had already returned, hair disheveled and eyes bright. They were all below deck by then, but she was not too worried. Daniel always went on long, solitary swims and he had told her once, "I will always come back, baby." But it was getting late, and the food was almost ready. She looked up, the chef still behind her giving her last-minute advice on how to hold the knife, and that's when she saw him. He was leaning against the galley door, arms crossed over his broad chest, smiling, looking at her. His goggles hung like a shining necklace around his neck. She smiled back to him with her eyes. She pointed to the chef who was still all eyes on her and the cucumbers. Aww! How she makes me happy, he thought. Bringing his hand to his mouth, he coughed lightly, and the chef looked up—frozen when he realized who was there looking at him.

"Can I borrow my wife back, please?" said Daniel. And not waiting for an answer he added, "Lunch in thirty minutes sound about right?"

"Y-Yes, sir," mumbled the young man, hands on a pan now, moving with the speed of someone caught but not punished.

"You devil, you!" said Daniel to Shari as they reclined on the master suite bed. "You have no idea what I do for you and

how much I love you." And then he kissed her, his tongue finding the softest of passages to the onset of her soul. His teeth
biting her lips with the tenderness of a mother lion to her cub,
eating her alive. And she tasted the sea in his mouth and on
his skin as she licked the dry salt from every hidden crevice before she mounted him and let herself go.

"So you like our chef," he whispered as she leaned close
to his mouth.

"Yes," she said.

"Will you fuck him for me?" he asked.

"Yes, if you want me to."

"But do you want to?" he asked.

"Do I want to?" She had not actually thought about it,
but suddenly she recalled the pressure of the chef's strong hips
against her sarong—his bulge a promise of youth and vigor.

"Do you want to? Would you like to do it?" he asked
again, breathing heavier.

"In front of you, yes," she said, and then she came in one
wave of silent pleasure after another. She was far too con-
scious to let the moans grow loud but she she could not stop
her legs from quivering—and the boat shook.

Once he was done as well, taking her from behind and
mimicking a naked version of what he had captured in the galley earlier, he told her about swimming through the underwater
tunnel and how he had been scared mainly about losing her.
But also that, by doing it, he knew that he had bought more

time for them to be together.

That is when she showed him, on her phone screen, a fantastic picture of him, in the distance, as if standing on water with arms stretched out in joy and defiance to the blue skies.

"A great picture," he said.

"Yes, it's already got a ton of likes on Instagram!" she laughed.

EIGHTEEN

T HEY SETTLED DOWN FOR LUNCH. The day was still young, but so much had happened in the last few hours that yesterday's dinner at the pier seemed like an eternity ago. Daniel remembered a colleague of his, who had been trained in the army, telling him, "You can do a lot in thirty seconds. You can change a life in thirty seconds." Yesterday was eons gone, a multitude of "thirty seconds" ago. He was happy his life had not changed dramatically. The only thing that counted for that moment was the love of his wife and the love he gave her. Yesterday's sex was gone, and she was still there, in front of him, at the other end of the rectangular table, smiling at him through her long eyelashes. Her gaze, directed straight at him, was as pure as the early light of the new morning.

She was so happy that they were all seated together in the middle of the boat in a tranquil bay, protected from the world. Happy also to have the other two girls on either side of her. Even as a little girl she had wanted to sit at the end of the table, but her father would always shoo her off. So eventually she'd gone away, left that table, left her country, and now she was sitting there while her sisters back home were still in the same place.

The sun made its presence felt as it heated her naked back through the white cotton tarp that shaded them. She loved that, loved feeling that heat. She looked around and saw how beautiful the table was, lined with colorful ceramic dishes containing all kind of salads and tomatoes. She tasted the fish the chef had barbecued on wood-chip coals. Simply delicious. She looked up at Daniel again. With a nod, he made her look back. There was the chef, coming to check on things. She smiled at him. "A toast for the chef," she said raising her glass. "Here, here!"

In one voice they all answered "Salud!"

She took another look at the young man, white apron covering the goods, and then turned to her husband, who was almost laughing, observing her. In the most seductive way possible, she brought her glass to her mouth and showed him how she could finish the clear wine in one long slow sip.

She was surrounded by heat—the sun, the gaze of her husband, the close presence of the ladies talking to each other across the narrow table, and the alcohol making its way into her. The young chef's stare added to the heat as she felt his eyes lingering on her back a little longer. She turned around again. "Amazing job," she told him. "I'm sure you have special tricks for dessert!" And turned back to the table. Jim and Alexander, facing each other at the other end of the table, were in deep conversation, something to do about ice fishing. She could only hear snippets of it. Closer to her, Julie was explaining to Angelica the merits of taking pictures on film rather than digitally. Shari looked up at Daniel again. He was sitting peacefully at the other end of the table, the true balance of her own presence. The guide to her life really, even though she did as she pleased. She realized they would not do anything, not even touch the young chef today, but later, at a much later time, he would come up again in passionate conversation with words whispered in the darkness of parted sheets. She knew she had to get to know the boy better to satisfy Daniel's insatiable appetite for stories and details. She had time, though—plenty of half minutes before the end of the day and their trip.

She looked around the table. They were all so far away from home, from the grid. Nobody could ever take moments like that away from them. There lay the value of wealth. She looked at Daniel again, talking to the other men now. He looked so good, she thought. And then she realized that it was her heart talking, not her eyes. He was handsome alright, but not like Jim, not even like Alexander. They had the beauty of youth and carefree existence. Daniel, on the other hand, had the beauty of a life lived and the strength of wealth. She wanted that in a man. It may not sound appropriate these days, in this era, yet she knew it was what she needed. Long ago she had noticed the difference between happiness and joy. She might not be able to spread happiness always, but she could spread joy. *"Simcha,"* Daniel called it using the Hebrew word. And she did, sharing her good fortune with the ones around her and creating moments of pure pleasure for all. It was in that architecture of the instant that she felt fulfilled as a woman. Her being translated itself on the surface of her behavior in the sweetest of demeanors. Her outer beauty was a true reflection of the purity of deeper thoughts, her body afloat among the sea of perceived desires. And if Daniel wanted it a certain way, then she would oblige. So much so that when she went back to the kitchen galley to help with the coffees, she could not help but stroke, with the gentlest of touches, the fabric that covered the bewildered chef's anatomy. She intended to take measure of his fullness so that later she could retell the story for Daniel's avid ears. Little did she expect the amplitude of her touch and its immediate consequence. She checked again. This time the young man had to shift the fabric to accommodate the full extent of his excitement.

The tray trembled a bit in her hands as she brought the six hot espressos back to the table. Only Daniel noticed the tremor. He watched the silver tray capture a sudden ray of light, like a wink from an angelic presence. Shari's hands never shook. "She could have been a surgeon," he sometimes said. He knew something had just happened back in the galley, the same way he knew whenever she left the house with more makeup than usual. She did it for him, and he had unleashed it after all. So he lived with it. For it.

She took a sip of the coffee, keeping her cup as steady as possible. What she had felt with her hand in the galley moments ago was not hardly as impressive as what the chef had actually shown her right after, unbuttoning his pants with one pull. "Now that was a sight to behold," she reflected. He had not even been fully erect, and yet she had understood the weight of its potential impact. She shyly smiled as he readjusted himself and she walked away balancing the tray.

What to do now? If she told Daniel the story, he most likely would want to hear more, to hear what else she had done. But she perceived this now almost as an act of infidelity, not just the occasional distraction she offered him from time to time. If anything was to happen with the chef, it was going to be a whole different experience. She felt as if time was flowing too slowly. Maybe if they were almost home, there would be no dilemma. But they were still hours away from returning. Which left her with hours to relive in her mind the invitation that stood beneath the white cotton pants.

"What do you think about taking selfies?" Angelica asked her.

"You can never take enough," she answered as a joke. She was not sure the ladies caught the forced frivolity of her answer, but they kept talking to each other, which allowed Shari one more thought. If she ever, ever did it with him, she'd need a picture of it, or Daniel wouldn't believe it. She stared out at the distant splash of the waves.

They all got up from the table, bodies and limbs aching from sitting too long after all the activities of the last hours. Julie and Jim settled in a hammock on the aft deck. Angelica fell asleep almost at once in a cozy corner of shade. Both Daniel and Alexander got on their phones to work, and Shari was left alone on the deck. Lying down on a towel, the sun was only a caress as the boat sailed away. She looked up and lost herself in the motion of the white sail stretched high above her. Everything around her seemed to beckon her to make the next move—the warm teak of the deck on her naked back, the heat of the wind along her legs and thighs, the smell of the sea that somehow now had a masculine imprint, and the motion of the boat that rocked her gently from side to side, the weight of her breasts dancing with the waves.

A vision of the chef's cock materialized from nowhere in the folds of the moving sails. She stood up, her body aglow with a thin layer of sweat, and walked silently past the two men who were too focused on their respective phones to notice. She went straight towards her cabin—mainly to splash her face with cool water and reassess her urge, but also to change into another somewhat sexier bathing suit. Just in case.

She quietly opened the door. And there he was, sitting at the edge of the bed, feet gathered and hands on his lap. Like a schoolboy, a good boy, waiting to be summoned. She smiled. There was little to debate anymore: The intruder was already in her cabin, and all that was left was to let him intrude further. For a split moment, she had thought about turning around and leaving, but she stood still. She took it all in, the honey-colored walls of the wooden cabin reflecting a glow of acquiescence, the way he had his hands on his lap, the quiet glimmer in his translucent blue eyes that brought the ocean into the room— it was all good. She followed her breath and, looking at him straight in the eyes, she untied the side ribbons that kept her bikini bottom on. In one swell move she brought her body, still warm from the sun, against the soft washed cotton of his trousers. She could feel the effect almost immediately—like sap flowing hard into his being. He was craving her, his hands, his mouth, his arms, they could not explore her fast enough. He was just unstoppable. She could feel his whole body tighten in a trance that went beyond definition, and she loved it. It was scary and intoxicating at the same time—his rock-hard belly lifting her up even before he penetrated her.

"Wait a second," she told him as she reached for her cell phone. She texted her husband, *If you want pictures, come to the cabin now with your phone.*

She tossed the phone to the side and told him, "Slow down,

sailor. I may have a guest come in, only to watch. But I don't want you to know who it is, so let me do this." She removed the top of her bikini, blindfolded him, laid him flat on the bed, his pants undone just wide enough for him to stand at full mast.

He started breathing heavily as she stroked him with the tip of her fingers. He did not hear the door open and close, never even knew that someone was watching, let alone recording. Shari, as if on cue, brought her head down, flicked her hair out of her face and licked the length of his massive cock while her hands coursed up and down all along it. She did not want him to come yet so, very slowly, she sat on it, facing away. It took her a moment before she could fully ac-commodate his girth. But she did. She knew she could do it. She did it for him. For herself. And for the camera and the cameraman. She could feel all their presence, mainly Daniel, who was facing her, as well as the lens of his camera that was recording all her moves, but also the chef's hands feverishly exploring her body and the anchored island of his cock which she was riding which such obvious pleasure. She let the shaft trespass her boundaries— it was the first time she had done it alone, face to face with her husband. Daniel looked at her as if in a trance, absorbing not only all the sights but also the sounds, the whisper of her pussy sliding up and down the cook's stiff cock and the hammer of his ever-louder breath. He even captured the faintest of smells in his state of heightened awareness, the sweet scent of her pleasure but also the pungent musk of his. Eventually, he looked up at her face. It was angelic, smiling and focused on him even as she stayed in constant motion. Their eyes locked, like accomplices. They both sensed that the young man could hold no longer. She moved away, just in time for his cum to strike her hard, like white lava, all over her chest and neck.

NINETEEN

ANIEL WAS ABOUT TO LEAVE but he had to press *Record* again when he saw Shari lean over and suck, from the still throbbing sex, the last seminal drops. Her mouth licked the shaft clean as she looked straight at the camera, her face identical to what it had been at lunch, when she stared at Daniel while she defiantly finished her glass of wine. Their eyes met one more time as her mouth finally took the whole tamed cock in.

Daniel softly closed the cabin door behind him, walking away as if stepping out of the haze of a dream. He took a few more steps into the main living area and found refuge on a sofa by the windows. He sat there alone, his gaze fixed on nothing for what appeared like a myriad of long seconds until he reached for his phone, holding it as you would a buoy in the middle of a long ocean swim. He pressed the replay button and saw the whole scene all over again— but this time he was the one whose hands were shaking. Even though he had just seen the whole thing with his own eyes, the recording on the screen made it all seem so much more real. He was mesmerized by it, and he watched it over and over, almost as a buffer.

So enthralled was he that he did not notice the crouched figure standing behind the windowpane. Alexander had taken refuge there from the sun when he heard the thump of the sofa against the tinted glass. He had turned around and suddenly was faced with the sight of the lovemaking on Daniel's phone. He too had glimpsed Shari's hips move up and down on the man's cock. He knew that Jim was still out on the deck with Julie, so he reckoned this must have been one of the crew members. The chef, if he had to guess. He wanted to look away, but he simply couldn't. There was no doubt to Alexander that this had just been filmed—he could make out the cabin in the background. He wanted to see the whole scene again, and Daniel obliged, playing the video over.

Alexander smiled when he realized that he was now the "voyeur of the voyeur." He was worried, though, that Daniel could turn around and notice him, so he retreated very slowly from the shaded spot. As he returned to the main lounge, he reflected on how bizarre it was to know that Daniel was actually watching his own wife being fucked. The man's face, illuminated by the screen, had been relaxed—almost serene, thought Alexander. Daniel had switched to the other video, the shorter one with Shari licking the lingering drops while she looked at him, her large dark eyes like pools of loving water. She had flickered her eyelashes. With love for himself, Daniel knew. But maybe also for that giant cock, he snickered. By then he was growing impatient to see her again.

It was one thing to see the pictures she had sent him in the past, when someone else took the shots or videotaped her. It was another when he was the one doing the videotaping, capturing the act. This was different also from the previous night, when everyone was doing everything to everybody. Then, he had been a link in a chain of stories, a man with a role to play. But in the cabin, he had been a passive observer, distant and somehow detached. He felt as if he had lost an edge and that by doing what he did, he had become a secondary player.

But how come he loved it so much? he wondered. How he had loved watching her tongue collect the last drops, running them along her lips as if teasing him. Maybe they were at it again, he thought, realizing that her invitation to "come to take pictures" had felt almost like an afterthought. She was going to fuck the chef either way and, if Daniel wanted to, he could "come take pictures." She had not asked him to come and fuck her with the boy. She had simply said, "If you want to take pictures, come now."

He could feel a distant emotion swell in him, that feeling of jealousy he thought he had completely forsaken. There it was, building up. It was not perhaps the worst feeling, but he wanted no part of it. Jealousy led to despair. He took a deep breath, collected his thoughts, and remembered the old book he traveled with. Observe your feelings, it had said. Be aware. Robert, an old Brazilian friend, had also told him once, long ago, "O.B.A.": Observe. Balance. Accept.

Well, that was all very nice and everything, but he suddenly grasped that he could not go beyond the "O". He could Observe, for sure, but that only led to pangs of jealousy—brewing jealousy that was swelling up like water in him. He stood up abruptly, hardly noticing Alexander, and went straight to the cabin. Maybe they were still fucking in there, he thought, almost out loud; and although that would have sounded lovely if retold in the depths of the night, under the sheets, with candlelight flickering in sync with the chill music, it was more than he could take right now.

He would soon find out.

He was not sure what he would do if he saw the two of them going at it again. On any other day, he would have joined them in his mind, willingly joined the act of providing the most immense pleasure possible to his wife. But clearly, he was not in a "sharing" state of mind just then. He had no violent intentions, no thought of punishing anyone. He was just curious about what was happening at that moment. About this life. About his wife.

He opened the door very slowly. Its corners had rounded

edges. His hand rested on the wood, the smoothness of it appeasing him a bit. It was very quiet in the cabin, and in the center of the bed lay Shari, alone and asleep under the smoothed-out sheets. Her moist lips were partly opened; mere moments before, he had seen them distended under pleasure. He kissed her with his eyes.

Balance.

Accept.

He was ready. And he closed the door, letting the smooth edge meet the smooth opening.

TWENTY

LL THE OTHERS WERE SLEEPING; only Alexander and Daniel remained awake. They were standing side by side on the edge of the boat, lulled by the motion of the waves and looking straight out into the infinite complexity of the ocean—always the same, always different, as a brain is a myriad of thoughts that percolate and percuss against each other toward an always-changing horizon. They both remained silent, elbows resting against the guardrail, lost in thought.

It was Alexander who broke the silence. "I may never have an opportunity to ask this again, but without going into details, how was it last night? I mean, when all of you. . . ." His voice trailed off as he let the sound of the water against the boat fill the silence.

Daniel did not shift from his position. He was thinking fast, because the longer it took for him to answer, the less authentic he knew it would sound. He answered with only one word, "Fantastic."

They fell silent again. "Like only a fantasy can be," he added. "That was all it was, Alexander. A fantasy. A unique coalescence of dreams and myths come true. Nothing to do with reality. Or truth. Or virtue, for that matter. Don't judge it. . .or her."

Alexander turned his back to the sea and leaned against the wooden rail, his face intermittently washed by the sun as the sail shifted in the wind. "I know," he said. "I just wanted to ask you. You seem so mature when it comes to these matters."

Daniel frowned a little. What did that mean? he asked himself. But he also realized that answering would open a whole new conversation. So he remained silent for a while, and then, turning to face the sun as well, he said with a smile, "You bet."

They both laughed, not even really knowing why, just for the pleasure of it, of the moment. Angelica, who was still curled up in a sofa, stirred and woke up, stretching her limbs. She stood up, strolled lazily to Alexander, and wrapping her arms around his neck asked in a sleepy voice, "What are you laughing about?"

"We're just laughing at how happy we are to have you

here," Daniel told her.

They heard noises further down the deck, watched the hammock swing crazily for a bit before Jim fell out of it with a loud thud. They laughed some more and were all smiles when Jim, followed closely by Julie, came towards them muttering, "Hammocks and sex are just not compatible." Then they all sank down back onto the plump chairs and sofas, laughing.

"Where's Shari?" Julie asked.

"She was busy with the kitchen," Daniel said. "She's sleeping now."

"Not anymore," said Jim, and they turned to see her step out in the light, a straw hat covering her eyes, her beautiful lips a dark shadow of pink.

TWENTY-ONE

LEXANDER WAS STANDING by the open doors that led to a small balcony facing Place Vauban. They call those French doors, the ones that provide a wider view of the world when they open as a pair, leading to more light, more horizon. Outside, the Parisian day carried its own color. This early in the morning, it was gray with a twinge of pink. Gray suits Paris well, always has, ever since it grew up around the haze of its silver river.

The building was, not so long ago, home to Antoine de Saint-Exupéry. The plaque at the bottom of the outside wall said so. He figured the writer's flat must have been the one on the top floor, right above them. He looked up. In a corner of the cornice hung a small nest made of mud, built by swallows with earth and their own saliva, a marvel of a cocoon.

The birds kept coming back to it over and over, flying in every few minutes. In and out, and in again. He could almost measure time by this incessant motion, he thought, as much as he could by the sun traveling above distant Pont Alexandre III.

From the balcony, he could make out the sumptuous winged horses on the bridge's four corners, and it reminded him of the story of Apollo, the Greek god initially charged with leading the chariot of the sun along its daily course. His son, Phaeton, had tricked him into allowing him to drive the chariot for one day. It was an impossible task for a lesser divine mortal, and the day had ended in disaster when Zeus had to strike Phaeton down to prevent further damage. Apollo was so distraught at the death of his son that he abandoned the task of driving the chariot and gave it to his assistant Helios, who later became the sole driver of the Sun Chariot. The sole. The sol. In France, "le soleil," he reflected with a smile and a nod towards the top floor. Le Petit Prince would have liked that connection.

He went back to the bedroom. Angelica was still in bed, sleeping, her head deep in pillows. He stood there for a while, his eyes focused on her naked shape barely hidden under the thin sheet—and his heart suddenly beat faster when he saw her stir, face him, and smile inquisitively with her eyes.

"Did you go jogging?" she asked, her voice still raw from dreams.

"I just came back. It's cold out there."

"Come in and warm up," she said as she lifted the sheet for him.

"I'll take a shower first," he said.

"No, come now. Just like that!" She reached for his shorts and pulled him close. And closer, her mouth opening just enough in the early morning sun to accommodate his saltiness. She must have had some very sweet dreams indeed, he thought as his fingers found her ready and wet. Or was it his vestige from last night? From day one they had shared everything, even his cum. No questions ever asked.

She was rousingly beautiful in the filtered morning light, and soon he was in her again. Her head arched back under his weight, revealing the tender softness of her neck. "Harder," he heard her say, and he reached deep and went faster, and deeper, and soon they were both riding the same wave, both transported to a place where the only thought remaining was to share each other. In that moment the rhythm of their joined breath became a bridge, a pathway made of air that linked them as close as flesh could be on flesh. Gradually she heard him exhale louder and louder, and her words—"fuck me, fuck me!"—resonated in the air around them until she too followed him into the purest of pleasures.

And then, interlaced together, they fell asleep as if ancient lovers from eons ago. Outside, the swallows continued their silent dance, flying quietly back and forth to the hollow nest, measuring a time that had no frame.

As he woke up, his bliss slowly lifted like mist evaporating on the side of a mountain. He found himself facing thoughts that had been percolating in his mind over the last few days. How did she do it? How did it feel? How did she like having the other men and their women all at once? How could she have done it?

Shari had been somewhat vague when she described the events of the night that preceded his arrival on the boat, but she had answered the few questions he asked.

"Where did it all happen?"

"Back here." She had pointed to the lounge area.

"Were there any crew members involved?"

"No, the crew was all gone by then. The boat was ours alone."

". . .Did it last a long time?"

Shari thought about it for a moment. "Spare no details," Angelica had said.

"Well, we slept in between. But then it happened again. A second time."

And it was that "second time" that really got to him. Slowly, achingly, within the deepest recesses of his mind, he was trying to reconfigure the sequence of events on the boat. The shapes remained out of focus, and the flesh in his visions was ill-defined but the overwhelming intent was clear. It was like watching distant stars, barely able to keep them in focus, yet the light, streaming through space at dizzying speed, ultimately reached you all the same.

"Time for breakfast," she said as she stretched out in bed and kissed him tenderly. She got up. He joined her just a little later in the warm shower, rinsing off the sweat of the run and the remains of the sex, as well as the new pervasive thoughts.

They went out to the local cafe where they were known by then. "Deux café et un croissant?" asked the waiter.

"Oui, Monsieur!" answered Angelica with a smile she very well knew would melt him away. She could not help herself. It was her nature to seduce, even there at the counter. This was her *raison d'être*—to seduce, and maybe let someone seduce her in return. She seduced all the time. She seduced in her walk, in the movement of her hips that oscillated from one contrapposto to the next—each step slicing space in a motion that spelled desire. She seduced with her mouth, lips full and willing, welcoming. With her deep brown eyes, deep like a bottomless lake, where, if she wanted you to, you could dive and get lost forever. She seduced because she liked it. She had been given the tools, and she was going to enjoy them, whether the weight of her lips against Alexander's or the spread of her hips under his kiss.

They spent their days walking along the Paris streets, discovering new ones every day. Alexander photographed her at all times, as if he was unable to get enough of her. He captured her smile growing larger on the screen as she walked towards him, or her silhouette as she navigated the cobblestones with a grace available only to those who had worn high heels all their lives. He painted her with photos, imprinting her image against the worn stones of ancient buildings.

Centuries ago, she might have been a courtesan there, with her breasts pushed high in tightly laced, corseted dresses, but they were free just then and almost visible under the weave of the black wool sweater she wore for him. He loved that sweater. In the right light, it captured her shape—her nipples like dark cherries under the stretched yarn. He waited for the sun to strike her just the right way and tripped the shutter over and over again, to the point that he fell in love with the images on his screen as much as with the real woman, all of her melting into his own light.

Paris had never looked so beautiful, and there was rapture and delight in each step as they moved in unison along the lanes. They moved as only lovers can, body against body, shape on shape. Once in a while, he would look up at the sculptures on churches, on palaces, and old buildings. There, he saw bodies of stone with limbs that twisted and met, and the hardness of a core that danced within soft curves. That is when, at times, for a fleeting instant, he had visions of real bodies of flesh superimposed upon each other and inter-twined—right there, on the deck of a boat. The boat. With Angelica in the midst of it. It was all too much. Even with all his love for her, every single time it appeared, he had to physically shake his head to spill the image out. He didn't want to think about it anymore, or for it to keep coming back to haunt him. And yet it did, insidiously, random images, one after the other at random moments. Her body naked among the four others. Her beautiful body, touched and taken, touched and tasted. The vision froze in his head, and he saw it again and again along the streets of Paris. He saw it even when he purposely avoided looking at the sculptures. The mere presence of columns around them were enough to stir the same emotions, as he saw them to be the many cocks that she could satisfy.

That night he took her in public, on the balcony of their apartment. It was during that moment of day when the last light bleeds into the night. The glow of the apartment behind them illuminated them as if they were on a small stage—the outline of her willing body glowing and beautifully naked. He took her, like that, under the gaze of the occasional passerby who would either linger or pretend, in a Parisian fashion, to have seen nothing. A couple gazed longer than the other onlookers, and he moved Angelica sideways. With unspoken words he wanted his revenge, his own display of his possession of her. His shadow long and tall in the darkening sky, he took her over and over, and when he had enough, he moved back indoors and took her again on the silk sofa, her legs sprawled over him.

The lingering couple moved away.

The imperial blue silk of the sofa slowly got stained under her liquid passion.

TWENTY-TWO

ESPITE THE RECURRENT VISIONS, HE WAS, most of the time, utterly fine and loving. As young lovers do, he enjoyed anticipating her needs and complimenting her. She loved all of it and loved him in return. Regardless of the weather, he took her by the hand and led her through Paris into hidden museums and nostalgic parks. He showed her a city that reveals itself only to those who take the time to look at clouds as if they were passing emotions and find hidden harmonies in the patterns of cobblestones. In return, she took to him with passion, just as any woman in ancient Greece would take Alexandros Paris, the beautiful son of Priam.

Sometimes they got a glimpse of Helena. Somehow, she often seemed to find a way to be where they were, as if to rectify destiny and let Paris steal her all over again. But he had eyes only for Angelica, his muse, his princess. Soon he bought her another beautiful vintage bracelet, and now she wore both, almost as a testament of her willingness to give him everything he desired—her lips, her appetite, her skin even as he struck it with soft lashes of his belt, and her ass as well if he so desired. Even her soul, if he demanded it. He had her completely and utterly, and she gave in, with feelings that she had never ever experienced before, to the sweetness of his fresh love and the embrace of a city that loves lovers more than any other capital. The streets moved forward with them, the avenues spread themselves as they entered, and every building reflected the love gleaming in their eyes. The light was good in the morning for lovemaking and at night for fucking, and they did both— eating when they were hungry, sleeping when tired, and drinking from each other whenever one wanted. . .and want they most often both did.

He realized that her body was the one he had secretly imagined ever since he was a child. Her breasts had forever filled his hands and his fingers had shadowed the shape of her thighs in the sweet air of dark nights long before he got the chance to trace them with his tongue. He knew the hills and valleys of her shape as if it had always been an icon floating ahead of him, waiting to come alive when lovingly beheld. The mere presence of her essence led him along a path barely traveled. Barely there. And within their shared moments of ecstasy, he would experience her body as a marvelous glass-like apparition, something out of this world, a fragrant incarnation. Yet at times, lost in an "out-worldly" union and linked in a state of effortless bliss, he would sense the definite weight of distant flesh. Always the same. The five of them, without him, in the back of the boat. That vision gradually becoming so vivid with time and repetition that it morphed into a detailed photograph in his mind. With lips bitten, tongues intertwined, and passions captured in flesh.

THEY WERE HAVING DINNER AT LE DUC, his favorite fish restaurant in Paris, where the waiters treated him with an affection proportionate to the beauty of the women he brought with him. That night, the fish he ordered for them was incredible—light and cooked to perfection, with a sauce that added the perfect weight to the palate. The Sancerre he ordered was called La Poussie, a name that made him laugh as he watched her drink it with a coy smile.

"The last time I had fish this good was on the boat in Cadaqués," she said innocently. All of a sudden, his breathing stopped. Of course! The boat! That is where their true love affair had started, but it also had been the receptacle of her debauchery, when he was not even there yet to witness it, to see her do the things that now could occur only in his mind. He took a long sip, letting the wine find its way into the depth of his being, as he heard Daniel's voice resounding in him. "Fantastic," he remembered him saying.

Fantastic.

Alexander kept silent, distant, oblivious even to the touch of Angelica's hand stroking his thigh.

"Are you alright, my love?" she asked him.

"Yes, I guess I am," he sighed.

"What's on your mind?" she asked again.

"It's just that. . .that I cannot stop thinking about the night before." The words came out slowly. "On the boat. You know? When the five of you were together. . . . It's stronger than me," he added softly.

He swirled the wine in his glass slowly, as if his entire being was focused only on the motion of the liquid in the crystal. "It keeps coming back and back, and I just do not know what to do with it, you see?" he finally blurted out, sounding more hurt than angry.

She stayed silent for a while and then in a soft, calm voice said to him, "If you want to, if it makes it easier for you, I will do it again. For you. With you, this time."

And as he looked at her stunned, she added, "Or without you, whichever you prefer, *mon amour.*"

The glass went straight back up to his lips and he drained it, a giant flow of emotions coursing through him. Excitement, bewilderment, fear, incomprehension—they were all jammed up against the roof of his mouth as if he needed to slowly swallow them one by one in order to digest what she had just proposed. How could she talk like that? How could she offer it, offer herself up that way? Did she want to lose him? To end it all? And then he looked up and saw her eyes looking deep into his, and in them, the depth of everlasting love and admiration. In that instant, he needed that silent gaze more than anything.

He started eating again, silently. Thinking and trying to focus on the pleasure of every bite. And then he looked up again and whispered, "Do you mean it?"

"I do if you want me to. If it is a burden for you, then this will be my gift to you."

He let the matter drop. They finished the bottle and had the Baba au Rhum for dessert. It was moist and soft and dripping with sweetness.

TWENTY-THREE

THERE WAS SO MUCH TO THINK ABOUT. He ran with it for a couple days, taking her words along with him during the long-distance runs he did to get ready for the upcoming New York City Marathon. Her voice swirled in his head as he ran: "Or without you, whichever you prefer," each syllable imprinting itself in his brain. It revealed a true insight into the dilemma he had been living with. If this inconceivable act was ever to happen, if he ever was to be with her together with multiple partners, would he want to watch or would he want to be a part of it? These were two very separate commitments, he realized. As the action unfolded, he could either get absorbed by another woman and the charms she had to offer, or his attention could remain entirely riveted on Angelica as he watched whatever happened to her—as if he was admiring a great work of art that he only partially owned.

Ever since he met her, he had been over the moon with Angelica, and she provided all the physical excitement he could need, so the idea of another woman in the mix was not something he was open to.

He slowly came to the realization, miles and miles of running later, that she was right. That he might choose for it to happen without him. It was amazing to him that he could even think in such a way. His thoughts had evolved from flashes of visions of the events on the boat to this elaborate conception of something that could potentially happen in his own reality. He ran faster. He realized that what had happened on that boat was much more than just sex. There had been layers and layers of drama, of melded stories, that affected him. He remembered Daniel and how he had described the prior night's events as "fantastic and out-worldly." He also recalled seeing Daniel watching the video of his wife fucking the chef. Funny to think that it was the same chef who had cooked the fish that Angelica liked so much—the fish that prompted his whole conversation with her to begin with. Full circle.

He ran faster and faster every day, yet he remained confused. The seconds he was shedding from his seven-minute-mile pace seemed to only add weight to his thoughts until he reached a point of clarity. He was running 6:30 splits and in the midst of the third one, he knew what he would do next.

The bedroom of Place Vauban had red curtains, and when

they were drawn a marvelous crimson hue would fall on the white sheets of the large bed. It was especially true in the early morning, when the sun, rising above the rooftops at the other end of the long esplanade, flooded the windows straight on. Almost instantaneously, the white room became magical. It was in that moment, while deep in her, that he whispered to her, "I want to take you to a special club."

"Which club is that, darling?" She could feel him getting even bigger, moving faster.

"A club where everything goes. Here, in Paris." He paused, and then added, "Would you go with me?" His voice was raspy as he spoke, his thrusts slow and deep, as if punctuating his words. "You can only go in as a couple, and there's a selection process at the door, letting only certain people in." He had slowed down a bit, his breath heavy. "Would you go with me?"

He waited, his heart leaning against her words. She did not have the heart to tell him that she had been there before, not so long before, when she was modeling in Paris and her job required her to be present, if not available, at all kinds of crazy parties.

In the sweetest voice possible she answered, "Whatever gives you pleasure is fun for me."

"You would go?" he asked again, moving faster now.

"Yes, my love. For you, yes." Her breasts heaved with his thrusts, and the words escaped out of her. "And I will do anything you want me to do," she added, measuring the power of that last sentence by the abundance of his cum all over her naked, crimson-colored body.

The beauty of a fantasy, its intrinsic power, is that it doesn't need to ever happen at all. They rode that wave for the longest time, surfing on words of decadence—of what she would do once they got to the club, of how many men she would entertain and satisfy so that he could indulge with their women, of how she would dress in order to let fingers find her, of garters and see-through outfits, of gorgeous black-strapped high-heel shoes that would stab at willing bodies and be destined to point to the skies. And each time he would come harder and harder, the thoughts untethered, the fantasy meeting the "fantastic."

He never mentioned the names of the other two couples of that fateful night on the sailboat. He never spoke to them, although he knew that Angelica chatted with the women from time to time. In his mind, he was going to take Angelica to the club after he was done running the New York City Marathon. In preparation, he learned more about the club from a friend who told him about the layout of the place and its tacit rules of engagement.

TWENTY-FOUR

THE WALLS WERE LINED with deep red velvet. Glass chandeliers and mirrored balls barely lit the dance floor where couples could be seen dancing—all seemingly trivial, if it had not been for the beautifully sexual outfits the women wore. Some of them were pros, others wives, and all were game. From that room, his friend told him, a pathway led to two darker secluded areas, more like underground caves, filled with low sofas and beds that fit every desire and number. You could just watch, or you could try to engage. Words were not spoken, only moves occurred, touches, glances, as countless scenarios folded and unfolded.

Whenever Alexander thought about the club, it stood before him like a beacon, but also like an obstacle, a rite of passage he had to master.

Angelica never thought about any of that, and she continued to meet Paris through his eyes and hands, and loved it. But she also noticed the days getting shorter, and she knew that the city would soon be coated in a cold gray hue like wet steel. New York, with its spurts of brilliant sunshine, seemed more and more attractive as the days went by. She rejoiced at the idea of going back there with Alexander for the race and maybe longer, she sometimes thought.

Her own focus for the moment was on fashion. Through a book she found, she had rediscovered the clothes of Schiaparelli and could not get enough of them—the fabrics, the layering, the gold jewelry. That, and vintage Prada. She wore only those designers around town, and in the evenings when she and Alexander went out to dinner, sometimes with friends, sometimes alone.

The race in New York was on Sunday, and they were to leave Friday morning on Air France. Alexander was tapering his training before the marathon, and he could feel the added energy building in him, ready to be unleashed at the start of the race.

She could feel it too, in the way with which he took her at night, in the intensity of his kisses that were long and passionate, and in his hands that seemingly could not leave her body throughout the days.

He was stroking her thighs at Angelina's on Rue de Rivoli while drinking the thickest hot chocolate imaginable. She saw the heavy liquid chocolate stain his smile as he brought the white ceramic cup to his lips. Just as she looked lovingly at those full lips, she remembered, in a sudden flow of images, everything they had done together over the last few weeks. Of how he had seduced her against all odds after she had turned him down initially in New York City, and of their nights and days in the convent and the Colombe d' Or in the South of France, and then Cadaqués, and now Paris. His strong hands deliciously climbed the inside of her naked thighs. She only wore garter belts and silk stocking nowadays, partly for him, but also for her own pleasure and the memory of all the women who had done it before her. She loved his hands, with their beautiful long fingers and an elegance that hid how strong they really were. She wished now for them to find her, and she parted her legs a little more in an open invitation. But even with his body leaning all the way, he was still too far, so she pushed herself forward until he could really *really* feel her. She let out a moan that reached the neighboring tables. "The chocolate is just marvelous!" she sighed out loud, laughing. Soon he added another layer of taste as he let her lick his fingers dry in front of everyone. He could not help himself, and he took a picture of her parted red moist lips around his fingers before leaving the table and their bewildered neighbors. He quoted Emile Zola as they left the gilded rooms: "In my opinion, you cannot say you have thoroughly seen anything until you have a photograph of it."

They decided to go to Le Duc again that night. It was Thursday, their last night in town. Angelica was stunning that evening, and she knew it. Everyone at the restaurant turned around to see her when they saw other patrons looking in her direction. She wore a tight-waisted jacket of heavy black wool with intricate gold embroidery on the back as well as on the two front pockets. It loosely covered a black see-through silk shirt over a lacy black balconette. Her skirt had a long slit on its side, and when a step was wide enough, it would reveal a glimpse of the garters she wore. It was as provocative as it was discreet.

They sat at the corner table they liked, next to the giant bead from a rare Pacific tree that looked like the most gorgeous set of women's buttocks. *"Coco de fesse,"* the sailors had called it in olden times when, crazy with lust, they jumped in the surrounding Seychelles water, hoping to score with a mermaid.

Referring to the Syren, he spoke to her of the writer Lampedusa who had written a lovely short story called "The Professor and the Mermaid," an allegory of the search for a perfect woman. She hung on to his words and relished them, together with long sips of their usual Sancerre. He was so interesting, really, such a source of constant amazement. Intellectual but sexual, excited but reserved, elegant and enigmatic. She knew very little of his past or his family. They had no time for that, every moment pushing them forward towards a goal that had no shape or texture. She was the one filling that void with her shape, her texture, and the banner of her presence was sufficient for both of them to keep moving in unison. They seemed to be living amid a cello concerto, a sound so pure, so angelic yet so human, that even Aphrodite, goddess of seduction, could be fooled.

The food was delicious as usual, and the banter with the seasoned waiters made them laugh, and in that cascade of laughter, lips wide apart, she looked even more beautiful and desirable. Alexander could see it for himself, but also see it on the face of discreet gentlemen who stole glances or watched her move to the bathroom. Impulsively, he had just told her, "Let's go to the club tonight!" The words spilled out of him before he knew what he had said. She had smiled, taken her bag, and told him to wait as she stood up and went to the bathroom. It was a good thing she told him that. For a moment, he thought she was leaving the restaurant and him as well.

When she returned, he noticed the new red on her lips, more pronounced now, more red on purpose. It took him a short while to notice that the balconette was gone, and the gorgeous shape of her bosom was no longer concealed, the black silk enhancing her curves and darkening her nipples. He was speechless for a moment longer, and she loved that in him, too. He loved her, there was no doubt in her mind. And therefore, she loved him even more. They stayed for dessert. The club did not open till 11:00 p.m., and she loved the *îles flottantes* and their clouds of whipped egg whites adrift on a cream lighter than air. With each spoonful she let the silkiness stream down her throat—her eyes in his eyes, her jacket a little more open. He realized, as did the waiter and a gentleman next to him, and the one at the next table as well, that they were like dominos, falling one after the other to the charms of a living, walking mermaid.

From the street they walked into an antechamber that led to the club's main entrance. There was another couple already waiting, a young girl and handsome older man. She was scantily clad once she removed her overcoat. She looked quite sexy, thought Angelica, intrigued. It was strange standing there for the few moments before the door opened, as if together in an elevator knowing that, once out of it, all might possibly be permitted. The older man looked at Angelica, ventured a smile, but the club-door swung open and revealed a woman dressed in black. The couple must have been regulars because she greeted them with a smile and without a word let them in.

She looked at Angelica next. "Good shoes," she said, pointing to the dark green high heels. "You could have done with a better skirt," she went on, not appreciating the slit that went up to her upper thigh. Alexander was about to protest when Angelica removed the whole skirt altogether, revealing her naked legs laced by black garters and silk, and her ass split in two by a dark red thong.

154 / LEO BIRCH

"Red and green," Alexander said. "So complementary."
He smiled. Not waiting for a response, Angelica also removed
her jacket.

"Better," the woman said as she opened the door wider
and ushered them in.

With her clothes in the coatroom, Angelica strolled ahead
of Alexander down the steps and into the bar to the right. The
neutral zone, Alexander reminded himself, a little taken aback
by how comfortable Angelica seemed to be there, almost as if
she knew the place already. Was it possible that she *had* been
there before? he wondered, but he had no time to dwell on it.
The music was loud, the women were dancing, and soon he
had a tequila in his hand.

People gathered in pairs mostly, all different from each
other but all dressed as if going to the most delirious Eyes Wide
Shut party. Everywhere the atmosphere was electric with the
intensity of an excitement generated by the seemingly endless
possibilities. Alexander did not know where to look first. At
the women of course, some of whom were incredibly beautiful,
and none unsightly in the dim light. But his eyes also caught
the men with these women. He soon realized that, once you
seduced one person from a couple, the other half would follow.

Some couples looked great together; they danced as if this
was a normal club with no adjacent rooms full of surprises and
sexual activities. They looked like they could be friends of
theirs, up there, back in the so-called "real world." He heard

different languages in addition to the French. An exotic Brazilian couple, a timid Hispanic one. No one really talking to each other. Just looking. Just watching. Just gauging. Would she want him? Would Angelica want the guy? The questions ran in his mind as he played along with the game and let the second drink further dull his senses in an already altered perception. He even thought for a moment that he had recognized the silhouette of a woman hastening toward a back room. He could not tell who. Maybe no one. He dismissed it altogether.

He looked again at Angelica. Even with her clothes on, she would have been one of the most desirable women there. But sitting in garters with legs crossed and her shirt unbuttoned one more step down, she was the jewel of the red velvet room. "Come," she said, pulling his hand. "I cannot sit like this for much longer." He remembered the boat in Cadaqués. He remembered why he was there, and he followed her. His eyes fixed on her beautiful body as it swayed ahead of him, and he was happy to be at the end of her extended hand.

TWENTY-FIVE

THE LIGHTS WERE EVEN DIMMER in the adjacent rooms—bright enough not to bump into someone by accident but dark enough to hide, and contemplate all, in anonymity. It was the smell that hit him first—a faint scent of disinfectant, reminiscent of the swimming pools he used to go to as a child, back when his mind was focused on blowing bubbles of water ahead of his breaststroke, swimming after something he himself had created but was always a step behind.

It was a far cry from where his mind was now. And yet, the elusive bubbles were still metaphorically alive in this darkness. He was taken aback by the frenetic action unfolding all around him. There was a woman sitting on a man while being licked from behind by another, all the while taking a third person in her mouth. Moans were everywhere, mixed with the piped-in music. A number of men were half-naked; one was completely nude. Most women wore almost nothing, but all had their high heels on. Bodies were like flashes of pale light as they moved against each other, capturing pleasure here and there, legs opening, mouths closing, tongues vibrating. It was incendiary, as if a flame was coursing through all of them at the same time.

Alexander held Angelica by the shoulders. He saw others who held their wives from behind, offering them up, breasts exposed, legs parted, eyes closed. He saw some waving at him to come with Angelica to their corner where the action was already in motion and fucking intense. He was not shocked but in a state of semi-stupor. His hand drifted to her legs, and he reached for her pussy only to find another hand already there, heavy digits pressing themselves into her wetness. She looked up at him, her eyes questioning.

"Let's go to the other room," he said, more as an escape than from desire. In the other room, the other low sofas were also embroidered by bodies in various stages of nakedness. Again, he thought he recognized someone. He looked a little harder. Walking on her knees towards the open legs of another woman, under the spell of two young men looking at them, was Helena, clad only in high stockings and high heels. It was her for sure. He felt Angelica recognize her as well by the pressure she added to his hand. They turned around, left the room, and left the club.

TWENTY-SIX

E WAS STILL CONFUSED AT THE START of the marathon—-like a beautiful glass object with a veil of imperfection in it, an autumn tree waiting for the wind to blow its final leaves away.

The 59th Street Bridge is a turning point in the race. Although it's only a bridge, it seems never-ending as it stretches ever so gradually upward in silence. But then, you turn right on First Avenue, and the sound of thousands of screaming fans hits you like cold water on a hot day. Your pace gets lighter. The end is getting closer. No doubt you will finish the race.

Alexander was thinking of all of this as he ran along the left side of the avenue. He had arranged a quick hello from Angelica a little further up, around 79th Street. He wanted to show her how strong and fast he was. His stride grew longer, his feet came off the asphalt with more speed, more bounce. She was there. Radiant. Waving at him from a distance. He saw her, and next to her stood Julie and Jim, and Daniel, and Shari, cheering him on, willing him to go on with fists in the air, and bells and screams. They were like five fingers of a hand waving at him. He smiled back, brought his arms up, and kept running faster and faster to their delight. He had meant to stop and kiss Angelica. It did not happen, and he could not tell why. He just kept running, faster than his expected pace and against his better judgement. "Plan the race and race the plan," his coach Mike had told him. Well, that was not happening now, and the last few miles became very hard for him. His mind drifted further and further away. His soul seemingly releasing another layer. Shedding another illusion.

HE TOOK A SHOWER ALONE AT HOME. Angelica was waiting for him at Daniel and Shari's townhouse. A celebration was planned.

Come quick, Champion! she had texted. *You will love this place. The furniture is incredible! And they have caviar :)*

She knew he loved caviar.

She knew he loved her.

He walked to the townhouse, each step painful after the race. He kept moving forward, knowing how therapeutic the steps were at dislodging the lactic acid buried deep in his muscles. He had already smiled at how dark orange his urine had been, a reflection of the effort of running a sub-three-hour marathon. And now he smiled again, thinking how he would rehydrate with the magnum of cold Bollinger he was bringing with him.

TWENTY-SEVEN

THE DOORBELL RANG AT THE TOWNHOUSE. "I'll go," said Angelica. She opened the door. The magnum of champagne was resting on the floor. No trace of Alexander. First, she thought it was a joke, but then she also saw the photograph leaning against the green glass of the oversized bottle. She recognized herself. Behind it, Alexander had hand-written *Angelica at Angelina's, Paris.*

That was it.

Nothing else.

She knew.

She picked up the bottle, closed the door, and walked up the stairs, letting her bracelets fall one after the other down the steep marble steps.

As she re-entered the living room, the cello concerto was

playing its final notes. She stood at the door for a moment longer. A new song started playing. Bob Marley. "No Woman, No Cry."

Angelica silently swayed her head in time with the rhythm.

"I got it," she muttered as her finger absentmindedly traced the curve of the Ruhlmann cabinet. "Right," she whispered to no one.

ACKNOWLEDGMENTS

Big thanks to Anouk, Gabrielle, Hugh, Rachel, Renée, Gabriel, and Scott. And special thanks to Kite and Barry.